OVERTIME,
UNDER
HIM

Overtime, Under Him

N.J. Walters

Susie Charles

Jan Springer

POCKET BOOKS

New York London Toronto Sydney

Pocket Books
A Division of Simon & Schuster, Inc.
1230 Avenue of the Americas
New York, NY 10020

First Pocket Books trade paperback edition January 2008

POCKET and colophon are registered trademarks of Simon & Schuster, Inc.

For information about special discounts for bulk purchases, please contact Simon & Schuster Special Sales at 1-800-456-6798 or business@simonandschuster.com.

Designed by Jamie Kerner Scott

Manufactured in the United States of America

10 9 8 7 6 5 4 3 2 1

ISBN-13: 978-1-4165-7661-7
ISBN-10:   1-4165-7661-4

CONTENTS

UNMASKING KELLY

N. J. WALTERS

To my friends on the playground, especially Kelly, thank you so much for your unwavering support, your good humor and friendship. You ladies are the best!

Also, thank you to my new editor, Mary Altman, for your hard work and guidance on this first project we have ever worked on together. Mary, you made edits fun. Now that's a talent!

To my wonderful husband who is always supportive and loving no matter what I do. I couldn't do it without you.

ONE

KELLY ALLEN STARED AT her reflection in the bar window. She almost glanced over her shoulder to see if there was someone standing behind her, for the woman staring back was unrecognizable.

The wind whipped up, sending a gust billowing under her voluminous skirt. Batting it down with one hand, she gripped the lapels of her coat tighter around her upper body. She'd borrowed the coat from her friend and it was too small and didn't quite close properly. A shiver raced down her spine. It wasn't so much the cold, although it was a cool, damp night. It was more a combination of fear and anticipation that held her captive as she continued to examine the woman reflected in the window.

It was a shadowy image at best. The streetlights and the muted glow from the surrounding businesses were the only illumination. It had rained earlier in the evening but now it was just a light drizzle. Puddles filled the streets and Kelly curled her toes in her impractical high-heeled shoes.

Although the reflection was dim, she knew all too well what she looked like. She was still amazed at the transformation her friend

Lori had wrought in one afternoon. Kelly had curly, shoulder-length auburn hair that she usually kept ruthlessly pulled back in a severe bun, but Lori had styled the thick mass and added some kind of gel to it. Now it was artfully tousled, falling around her shoulders.

That wasn't all her friend had done. Kelly never wore much makeup beyond a swipe of mascara and a slick of nearly nude lipstick, but Lori had added eye shadow and eyeliner and now Kelly's blue eyes looked deep and mysterious. A touch of color on her cheeks actually made her look like she had cheekbones and a rich plum lipstick accentuated her full lips. It was amazing how some makeup and a new hairdo changed her look.

But Lori hadn't been finished by any means. Her friend had poked and prodded her until she'd donned the outfit that they'd decided on. Kelly hadn't been so sure, but her friend had been insistent, so Kelly had reluctantly squeezed her size sixteen body into a tight bustier and a many-layered skirt that fell to just below her knees.

The bustier was mostly black with red trim and laces running up the front. It cupped her breasts, pushing the already large 36 D-cup mounds even higher. Kelly had to fight the urge to keep tugging at the front of her top. She'd never worn anything cut so low in her life. If she bent over too far, she was afraid her nipples would show. But she had to admit that her cleavage was impressive.

The skirt was made of a silky material that matched the bustier. Layers of crinoline beneath it caused a swishing sound when she walked. A hint of red peeked out from beneath the hem of the skirt. Black fishnet thigh-high stockings and high-heeled shoes completed her ensemble.

Kelly was a tall, sturdy girl standing a shade below six feet in her stocking feet. With the three-inch heels that Lori had insisted she wear, Kelly felt like a giant. But even she would admit that she looked different. With her waist cinched in and her breasts accentuated, she looked, well, almost sexy. It was so unlike her that she'd kept checking the mirror at home until Lori had finally pushed her out the door and into the waiting cab.

Her fingers clenched as she pulled away from her reflection. Material crinkled as she looked down at the most important piece of her costume—her mask. It too was black and trimmed with red and covered most of her forehead and nose. Combined with her makeover, it would easily conceal enough of her face to mask her true identity. Without it, she'd never have the nerve to attempt what she was about to do. Placing a hand on her stomach to try to calm her jittery nerves, she took a deep breath and slowly released it. She, Kelly Allen, was about to walk into Brannigan's Pub and seduce the owner, Liam Brannigan.

Liam Brannigan was the stuff of women's fantasies. He had hair so black it looked almost blue in some lights and he wore it long and loose around his shoulders. His eyes were the same dark blue as a night sky and a perpetual shadow covered his chin, giving him a sexy, just-got-out-of-bed look that had caught more than one woman's eye.

And that was even before you got to his body. His shoulders had to be almost a yard wide and his massive chest tapered down to a lean waist. His legs were long and muscular and the way he filled out a pair of jeans ought to be illegal. At six-foot-four, he was even taller than she was. And in Kelly's experience, that didn't happen very often.

Just the mere thought of him had her breasts swelling and her nipples puckering. She could feel them pressing against the stiff fabric of the bustier and it took all her willpower not to press her hands against them to help ease the ache. Her panties were already damp with need. She could feel the cream slipping from her body as she pictured Liam in a pair of tight jeans and nothing else. Kelly gulped back air to try to calm herself.

She'd been working as a waitress at Brannigan's for more than a year now. Most people didn't seem to think of it as a profession but Kelly had long ago decided that, not only did she like it, she was proficient enough at it to make decent money. At twenty-six, she was settled and content with her life. She enjoyed her job, her friends and her hobbies. She didn't date much and hadn't had a serious relationship in two years. Most men were put off by her height, her weight or both. Kelly tried to convince herself that she didn't care but it still stung.

Brannigan's was a neighborhood pub. They opened at eleven, just in time for the lunch crowd, and closed at one o'clock in the morning. They served both lunch and supper—mostly sandwich platters and soups. The rest of the day, they served pub snacks. And, of course, the beer flowed freely all day long. It wasn't a rowdy place but, rather, a comfortable one. They had a lot of regular customers and were a favorite hangout in the neighborhood.

Personally, Kelly thought that many of the female patrons flocked there just for the chance to glimpse Liam. And who could blame them? Liam's good nature and his easy, friendly manner attracted both males and females alike, while his sheer size kept the occasional drunk or problem customer in line.

A door opened and closed and the noise from the bar filtered out onto the street. The annual Halloween Masquerade party was under way and had been for quite some time. It was already close to midnight. Liam hadn't been too happy with her when she'd asked for the day off, but since she'd worked all the holiday shifts since she came to Brannigan's Pub, he had agreed. She really hadn't liked leaving him short-handed for the party but Lori had insisted that she'd need the time to work her magic on Kelly.

In the end, Kelly had gone in at nine this morning and left at three in the afternoon. That way, she'd been able to take care of most of the preparations for the party as well as cover the lunch crowd. People had been in a celebratory mood during lunch and many of the patrons had been planning on coming back for the party. Several of them had asked if she was going to be at the party, but she'd told them that she had other plans for the evening. Liam had continued to scowl at her every time she'd said that. It had only added to her guilt.

But she'd done it anyway. It was her own fault she was in this predicament. One night not so long ago, she'd had one too many glasses of wine and spilled her well-kept secret to Lori. For more than a year, she'd secretly yearned to seduce her boss. It was more than just that, though. After working side-by-side with Liam for a year, Kelly knew that he was everything she'd ever wanted in a man. Hardworking and loyal, he inspired the same in his staff. His humor was infectious and he had a basic honesty about him that was very appealing. They shared many of the same views on things but had enough differences to keep it interesting.

But Liam was not a settling-down kind of man. At thirty-two, he owned his own business, had good friends and plenty of interests. He never lacked for female companionship but he never had a serious relationship. He worked hard and he played hard. The fact that he lived in an apartment above the bar meant that he worked long hours and he always teased that no woman would put up with that. But Kelly knew better. If there was no woman in his life, it was by his own choice.

That was fine with her. She was under no illusion that she could attract and keep a man like Liam, but she could take this shot at a one-night stand. Hot, grinding, sweaty sex was just what she needed according to Lori. And after many restless nights dreaming about Liam, Kelly was finally willing to agree with her. She might not get forever, but she would have this one night with him. That was, if she could work up enough nerve to open the door and go inside.

It had all seemed so simple back at her apartment with Lori goading her on—she'd dress up in a sexy outfit, put on her mask, saunter into the bar and seduce Liam. It was only now she realized just how many flaws there were in her flimsy plan.

Number one, she couldn't saunter in her high-heeled shoes. Used to wearing flats or sneakers, Kelly had been practicing walking in her shoes for days. But as hard as she tried, she still tottered on her heels. The first pair of shoes Lori had pressed on her had been a disaster. Kelly had been unable to even stand up in the four-inch, impossibly skinny heels. Lori had relented and they'd settled on a pair of black three-inch heels with open toes and a slender strap that wrapped around her foot. It had taken a lot of practice but at least she could walk in them, and even she admitted that they made her feel sexy.

Problem number two was she didn't really know how to go about seducing a man. Yes, she'd dated, but she'd never purposely set out to seduce anyone into having a one-night fling. In fact, she'd never had one in her life. The two men she'd had sexual relationships with had been men she'd dated seriously for several months before she'd actually slept with them.

And problem three was that underneath the sexy saloon girl costume, she was still Kelly Allen—tall, overweight and not very confident in the sexual arena. She chewed uncertainly on her lip and immediately stopped when she realized she was wearing away her lipstick. A part of her longed to run home, haul off the costume, and wrap herself in her flannel pajamas, but another part of her wanted to reach out and take a chance at getting what she wanted. And she definitely wanted Liam Brannigan. Besides, her cab was long gone and it would be almost impossible to hail another on a busy night like tonight.

A man in a cowboy hat, denim shirt and tight jeans sauntered by. He stopped, turned and stared at her, emitting an almost soundless whistle as he did so. Kelly was shocked when he slowly ran his eyes up and down her body. His lips turned up in a slow, welcoming smile. "Well howdy, sweetheart." He tipped back his hat with his index finger as his smile grew wider. "Are you going to the party?"

It was now or never. Slipping her mask down over her eyes, she adjusted it so that it was comfortable. In the soft, sultry voice that she'd been practicing, she smiled at the cowboy. "I believe I will."

He reached out and pulled open the door to Brannigan's, motioning her forward with a sweep of his arm. "After you, beautiful lady."

Placing one foot in front of the other, Kelly took the steps that led her from the cool, damp street and into the waiting party.

TWO

HE COMBINATION OF INTENSE heat, laughter and Celtic music assaulted her senses as she entered the room. Although the lights weren't bright, they seemed harsh after the darkness outside. She blinked several times before her eyes adjusted. A large hand pressed against the base of her spine, making her jump.

"Whoa there, sugar," the cowboy whispered in her ear. "Just don't want the crowd to run you over." It was a logical explanation, as the pub was packed to capacity, but Kelly could feel the heat even through the layers of her coat and costume.

Taking a tiny step away from him, she looked around the bar, a feeling of pleasure and satisfaction filling her as she watched the throng of people enjoying themselves. She and some of the other staff had worked all morning decking out the bar and it had definitely been worth all the time they'd put into it. Orange and purple lights were strung around the bar and carved pumpkins sat in the center of each table with lights shining through their slanted eyes and crooked mouths. Rather than hire a band, they'd had a DJ set up in one corner so that the music would be continuous all night long. The top of the pool table had been covered with a large, festive tablecloth that was loaded down with pub snacks.

"Can I buy you a drink?" Kelly was surprised that the cowboy was still standing behind her. She really looked at him for the first time and was shocked to find that he was actually good-looking. With his cowboy boots, he was as tall as she was even with her heels.

But as great as he looked, he wasn't the man she wanted. "Thank you," she began regretfully but he held up a hand to stop her.

"No need, sugar. I knew a fine woman like you had to be taken." Reaching out, he lifted her hand and brought it to his mouth. "But if he disappoints you, you just come and find me." He placed a soft kiss on her knuckles before releasing her hand, turning and blending into the crowd.

Kelly knew that her mouth must be hanging open but she couldn't help it. Men didn't flirt with her. They just didn't. But she'd seen the honest appreciation in his eyes as he'd stared at her. His actions bolstered her spirits, giving her a renewed confidence. Slipping off her jacket, she headed toward the bar. She was grateful for the long, red silk gloves that covered her arms to just above her elbows. The bustier left her shoulders exposed and the gloves helped her feel not quite so naked.

The room was crowded with people and it took her a while to work her way toward the bar at the far end where Liam was doling out drinks and conversation. An Elvis and a vampire waylaid her and it took her some time to convince them that she wasn't interested in their rather graphic proposals. Amused, perhaps, but not interested. Really, she'd gotten more indecent propositions tonight than she'd had in her entire life. She knew her outfit was sexy but this was just too much.

She heard him before she saw him. His laughter rang out across the bar, cutting through the music. The crowd seemed to part in front of her and she caught sight of him. She froze in place as he tipped back his head and laughed again at some jest a customer had made.

His long, black hair flowed down over his shoulders and she caught the glint of a diamond stud in his ear. The open neck of his crisp, white shirt framed the strong column of his neck. The shirt sleeves were long and billowy, ending in tight cuffs around his thick wrists. He looked every inch the pirate.

Moving like a sleepwalker in a dream, Kelly didn't quite know how she made it to the bar without tripping. She draped her coat over the back of an empty stool tucked away in a dimly lit corner on the far side of the bar. Sliding onto the seat, she propped her elbows on the edge of the bar, rested her chin in her hands and continued to stare at him.

His tight black jeans left nothing to the imagination, show-casing his muscular thighs and the impressive bulge of his cock. Black leather boots rose to his knees and he wore a dagger strapped to his side that looked incredibly real. The costume suited him perfectly.

She sighed as she ogled his tight butt, her fingers itching to touch it, and she had to swallow her groan of disappointment when he turned around again. Although the front view was even better than the back. Truthfully, the man didn't have a bad side.

Liam worked his way down the bar, serving up tall, cold mugs of beer and mixing drinks until he finally reached her far corner. "Welcome to Brannigan's, pretty lady. What can I get you?" His smooth, deep tones rolled across her skin like a caress. He stood in front of her with his hands on his hips and a twinkle in those deep blue eyes. His shirt was open at the top, emphasizing the strong column of his neck and offering her a tantalizing glimpse of his impressive chest. Really, the man was too sexy to be let out amongst the regular population.

She frowned when she realized he was staring at her. Glancing down, she had a quick peek at her cleavage to make sure she hadn't fallen out of the bustier. It was close. Her breasts swelled against the lace trim, but her nipples were still covered. Barely.

Her head jerked up when she felt his fingers beneath her chin. But instead of releasing her, his hand cupped her jaw and he leaned closer. For a moment she thought he might kiss her. Her lips parted in anticipation. His breath was warm on her moist mouth. He was close. So very close.

"What can I get you?" His voice was so soft and seductive it took a few seconds for her to process the meaning of his words. She jerked her head back in embarrassment, her cheeks heating. While she'd been all but undressing the man with her eyes, he'd been waiting for her to order.

"White wine, please." Her tone was briskly matter-of-fact and Kelly wanted to bang her head against the bar in frustration. She wasn't supposed to use her regular voice. She'd practiced lowering her voice and speaking more slowly and sensually.

But Liam had turned away to fill her drink order, giving no indication that he recognized her. Good. All wasn't lost. She could do this. She knew she could. When he placed her glass on the bar in front of her, she smiled at him. "Thank you, handsome." This time, her voice was mellow with a come-hither tone.

He smiled his pirate's grin. "You're welcome. You here with anyone?"

This was it. This was her chance. Trying not to seem too eager, she picked up her glass and took a long sip. Lowering the glass back to the bar, she licked her lips, allowing her tongue to stroke across first the upper and then the lower lip. His eyes tracked every movement of her tongue.

Was it just her or was the room getting hotter? Her costume suddenly seemed incredibly tight and she struggled to breathe. Her breasts felt so heavy and the tips ached unbearably. The tight lacing that cinched her waist and torso made her feel voluptuous and unbelievably sexy. Her pussy throbbed and she struggled not to squirm in her seat.

"No," she managed to whisper. "I'm not with anyone."

Liam leaned across the bar and stared into her eyes. The world around them disappeared. The sounds of the music, the chatter of the people and the din of the bar seemed to fade into nothing. There was only her and Liam. His lips barely skimmed hers before leaving a trail of hot, moist kisses to her ear. He traced the whorl of her ear with his tongue before nipping the lobe with his teeth. "You are now," he whispered. "If that's what you want."

Kelly gripped the bar with her hands to keep from slipping off her stool and melting onto the floor. Molten lava flowed through her veins. Need pulsed through her body unlike anything she'd ever experienced. Oh, yeah, she definitely wanted. She tried to speak but words were beyond her. She managed to nod her head in agreement but that was enough for Liam.

"Don't go anywhere, sweetheart." He gave her neck one final nuzzle before pulling away. "I've got to work but I'll be back."

Again, Kelly just nodded as he went back to serving up drinks. The pub's part-time bartender, Frank, joined him behind the counter and began to fill the waitresses' orders. Trying to regain her equilibrium, she turned sideways in her seat so she could watch the crowd. The waitresses moved easily through the throngs of people, carrying their trays loaded with drinks. She ruthlessly squashed her momentary feeling of guilt for not working tonight.

Resting one arm on the counter, she sipped her wine as she enjoyed the scene before her. The bar was alive with music and she tapped her toe as several lively tunes had the dance floor hopping. As the faster songs gave way to a slower one, the mood changed. Bodies moved closer, swaying in time. The lights flickered across many of the faces, giving them an exotic, otherworldly look. Hands groped and stroked as things got steamy between some of the partners.

Just watching them was making her hot. She could almost feel the stroke of a hand across her own back. Then she felt it again—a hard hand slid down the long line of her back, ending just above her behind. Startled, she whirled around, glaring at the offender. She'd been so caught up with the dancers she hadn't noticed anyone coming up beside her. It was her cowboy again and he was staring at her, totally unabashed and unrepentant.

"Hey, sugar. I thought you said you were here with someone." He laid his empty beer bottle on the counter next to her wineglass.

Kelly automatically glanced toward Liam and was surprised to find him only a few steps away with a scowl on his face. She hadn't realized that he was so close to her end of the bar. She opened her mouth to reply but before she could get the words out, Liam's deep, harsh voice cut her off. "The lady is with me." Kelly could only stare in wonder at Liam as he glared at the cowboy.

The cowboy stood tall and stared back at Liam, seemingly totally unafraid of his size or the potential threat he presented. Kelly could barely stand the tension that flowed between the two men. Finally, after what seemed an intolerable length of time but was probably no more than a few seconds, the cowboy tipped his head toward Liam.

Turning back to her, he smiled. Reaching into his back pocket, he drew out a business card and, without a word, tucked it safely into her coat pocket. As he stood, his lips grazed her ear. "Just in case it doesn't work out with him, sugar." He turned and sauntered toward the entrance, melting into the crowd. Kelly watched him until he disappeared from sight, catching a final glimpse of him as he opened the front door and left.

"Would you rather have gone with him?" Her attention snapped back to Liam, who was standing there looking like a thundercloud.

Kelly shook her head and licked her dry lips. "No. I'd rather be here with you."

"Are you sure, sweetheart?"

"Yes." Propping her elbows on the bar, she squeezed her arms against her sides, knowing that the simple action pushed her breasts even higher.

Liam's eyes glowed as he stared at the creamy mounds of her breasts. Her nipples tingled under his stare. "Prove it."

"What?" Now she was totally lost.

Liam leaned closer and ran a finger over the slope of a breast and dipped into her cleavage. Kelly didn't dare breathe until he'd withdrawn his hand. Her skin burned where he'd touched her. "Go to the ladies' room, take off your panties and bring them back to me."

"Are you nuts?" She was shocked and aroused by his suggestion. The conflicting emotions rocketed through her entire body. Her pussy was flooded with cream as she imagined herself seated on the barstool with no panties on.

"No. I want your pussy hot and wet for me by the time we close. I want you to want my cock in your body." His gaze scorched her with its heat. "I know your panties will be damp. They'll smell like you too—hot, musky and oh so inviting. You've already creamed your panties, haven't you, sweetheart?"

Kelly thought she'd come on the spot. No man had ever spoken to her in such a blatantly sexual manner before and she loved it. Determined not to let him totally have the upper hand, she parted her lips and flicked her tongue over her lip. "Yes, my panties are soaked." Her words were barely a whisper, but he definitely heard her. His eyes got even darker and he looked determined.

"I want them." His voice was thick with arousal. "You know you want to give them to me, don't you, sweetheart? Imagine how good you'll feel and how wet your pussy will get," he whispered as he leaned forward to trace the curve of her ear with his tongue. "If nothing else, it'll drive me crazy knowing you're naked underneath that incredible dress." He took a step back and she immediately missed his nearness. The corner of his mouth turned up in a grin but his eyes didn't reflect any humor. His entire body was tense as he waited for her decision.

Kelly had come too far to turn back now. She'd never seen Liam like this before, so blatantly sexual and demanding. While she had some experience in lovemaking, she'd never played sexual games with a partner before and found the possibility of indulging in them with Liam incredibly exciting and arousing. She wasn't about to stop now, not when she was finally so close to getting what she wanted.

Giving him what she hoped was a sultry smile, she slid off her barstool. "I'll be right back." Putting a sway in her hips, she walked toward the bathrooms. She could feel his eyes burning into her back with every step she took. When the door of the ladies' room closed behind her, she slumped back against the door. What in the heck had she just done?

THREE

LIAM WATCHED HIS MYSTERY lady leave, unable to tear his gaze away from the hypnotic sway of her hips. He could imagine gripping those hips from behind while he pounded his cock into her sweet pussy. He could almost hear the slap of his stomach against her ass as he took her. This was a real woman, full-figured and made to cradle a man of his size.

He'd noticed her the second she'd stepped through the doorway. She was tall and stood head and shoulders over most of the women and was even taller than many of the men. The light glinted off the reddish tones in her hair, making it shine like a jewel. And when she'd slipped off her coat, he'd almost swallowed his tongue. Her costume hugged her like a lover.

Her waist was cinched inward, accentuating the flare of her wide hips and the sheer magnificence of her breasts. The top of her outfit pushed her breasts high, leaving most of them exposed to view. Her creamy shoulders were bare but her hands and arms were covered by silky gloves. He'd never seen anything so sexy in his life. Just fantasizing about how that silk-covered hand would feel stroking his cock had caused it to swell to almost painful proportions. Liam had stuck close to the bar, trying his best to hide his erection from the customers seated there. He was thankful that most of them were wrapped up in their own business and were not paying him much attention.

No doubt about it. The lady was his and he hadn't hesitated to lay claim to her when she'd sat down. It had taken almost more restraint than he possessed to keep from hauling her up onto the bar, flipping up her skirt, pulling down her top and fucking her in front of everyone. He wanted to yell that she was his. He wanted to claim her in every way possible. And he damn well wasn't going to let some sweet-talking cowboy steal her away.

It was a good thing that he could practically tend bar in his sleep. He served customers and filled drink orders by rote, all the while keeping one eye on the door to the ladies' room. She'd been in there a long time. What if he'd pushed her too hard? What if she changed her mind? He'd almost lost it when the cowboy had left her his card and he had wanted her to prove that she belonged to him. Chauvinistic and primitive, he'd demanded her panties in compensation. Now he was afraid that she might run from him instead.

He heaved a huge breath of relief when the door finally opened and she stepped out. His mouth went dry as he imagined her flipping up the tail of her full skirt, hooking her fingers in her panties and dragging them down over her hips and legs. He could picture her bending down and slipping them over those sexy high-heeled shoes she was wearing. Had she really done it?

Yes, she had. He could tell by the nervous way she glanced around the room before heading toward the bar. Her legs were shaky as she wobbled on her shoes. He could see that her left hand was buried in the folds of her skirt.

Taking a deep breath, Liam forced himself to look away. If he wasn't careful, he'd come in his damned pants. His balls were so tight, he knew he was close. He was very aware of her smoothing her skirt under herself as she slipped back onto her stool but he continued to fill drink orders until he had some amount of control over his body again.

When he felt ready, he filled another glass with wine and placed it in front of her. "Compliments of the house, sweetheart." She nervously glanced around and chewed on her bottom lip. Liam wanted to howl with need. He wanted to lick that sweet lip before he claimed her mouth and sucked on that luscious tongue. "Do you have something for me?"

Her hand shot across the bar and he barely caught the small scrap of fabric before it slipped over the edge. Red satin filled his hand and he wrapped his fingers around it possessively. Angling his back so that no one could see what he was doing, he brought the fabric to his nose and drew in a deep breath. Her eyes dilated until they were almost black. He could see the arousal in her face and body as her breasts rose and fell quickly. Oh, yeah, his lady was as hot and bothered as he was.

"For now, it's your panties. I plan to touch and smell and lick your hot pussy as soon as this bar is closed." Lifting the wineglass in his hand, he brought it to her mouth. She parted her lips and swallowed as he tipped the glass up. "Your mouth is so damn sexy. I can't wait to feel your lips wrapped around my cock, sucking it hard." When he'd lowered the glass back to the counter, he gave her one last, long stare. "Keep your legs spread wide apart, sweetheart. I want you primed and ready. I plan on fucking you long and hard."

He glanced at the clock as he went back to work. Only a half-hour left until closing. His shout of "last call" had folks hurrying up to the bar. Although he was busy, he was very aware of the woman waiting for him.

KELLY ALMOST BOLTED AND ran before the bar closed, but she'd come too far and she wanted this so very badly. Even though she was decently covered, she felt totally exposed.

Her legs were hooked around the sides of the barstool so that her sex was wide open but the folds of her skirt covered everything. Her breasts ached and when she looked down she could just see the edge of two rosy nipples peeking up at her. She resisted the urge to tug at her bustier. In the dimly lit corner where she sat, no one could see them but her, or Liam if he happened to come over.

But he'd been busy since she'd shoved her panties at him. She still couldn't believe that he'd sniffed them before stuffing them into his back pocket. And the things he'd said to her had sent waves of desire pulsing through her body. She was more than ready to be fucked long and hard, as he'd put it, but she was determined to fulfill some of her own fantasies first. This was her one and only opportunity to be with Liam and she planned to make the most of it.

When the door finally closed on the last customer and the last of the staff had departed, Liam shot the bolts home and turned off the main lights. Only the candles sputtering in the pumpkins and the strings of orange and purple lights illuminated the room. Kelly had pushed off her barstool while he'd been ushering out the last person. She took the change that she'd fished out of her coat pocket and fed it into the jukebox in the far corner of the bar. Pressing several buttons, she waited until a low, sexy beat began to pound from the speakers.

The staff had cleared the remains of the food from the pool table so Kelly flipped back the tablecloth that covered it. Rolling the cloth into a bundle, she dropped it onto the floor.

Liam walked toward her with a predatory gleam in his eye. With his long, black hair and superbly muscled physique, he resembled a large jungle cat on the prowl and she was definitely his prey. Kelly was more than willing to be caught, but not just yet.

She positioned two chairs as he moved toward her. When he showed no sign of stopping, she held up both hands. "Wait." He froze in place, but she could feel the sexual energy vibrating from him. She took a deep breath and took the plunge. "I want to dance for you first."

LIAM STOPPED DEAD IN his tracks when she held up her hands and told him to wait. His hands clenched into fists at his sides and every muscle in his body was poised for action. Had she changed her mind? He didn't think so. Her body language and lustful stare told him otherwise. But still he waited.

Her words stopped his heart for a brief moment before it began to slam hard against his chest. *She wanted to dance for him.* That was something he really wanted to see. The pounding of the music matched his heartbeat as she made her way to the chair she'd positioned next to the pool table.

She raised one foot and placed it on the chair. Her skirt slid upward, revealing a long, lush leg covered in fishnet. He'd soon find out if she was wearing a garter belt or thigh-high stockings. His entire body tightened in anticipation. She bit her lip uncertainly and it occurred to him just how awkward it would be for her to climb in heels.

Hastening to her side, he offered her his hand. The smile she gave him was filled with sensual promise as she stepped up onto the chair and, from there, moved to the top of the pool table. Liam really didn't want to let go of her but did so when she gave her hand a slight tug.

"Why don't you have a seat, relax and enjoy the show?" She waved her hand toward the other chair she'd positioned about four feet from the table.

Liam strode to the chair and dropped down into it. Flicking open the cuffs of his shirt, he rolled up the sleeves. When he finished, he crossed his arms over his chest, spread his long legs out in front of him and hooked one booted ankle over the other. Cocking an eyebrow at her, he waited.

He could tell she was nervous but determined. At first her movements were a little jerky and shaky, but the longer she swayed to the music, the more fluid they became. Raising her shapely arms in the air, she swung her hips from side to side. Slowly, she lowered her hands, running them down her neck and exposed chest. The red silk gloves were in stark contrast with her pale skin.

Lovingly, she cupped her breasts in her hands. He could just see the tips of her nipples peeking out of the bustier. He licked his lips, longing to taste them, to suckle them, to pleasure them. Reaching down, he adjusted his erection but there was no comfort to be found.

Her clever fingers dipped into her bodice and flicked at the puckered tips of her breasts. She shivered with desire at her own touch. It was amazingly arousing to watch her pleasure herself but he wanted more. "Keep going, sweetheart," he encouraged.

She moved her hips enticingly with each beat of the music. Sliding her hands down over her torso, she gripped the sides of her skirt and, with each movement, pulled the fabric higher. Liam sat up straight and leaned forward as the tops of her stockings came into view. "I knew you'd be wearing thigh-highs," he murmured as she continued to tease him with glimpses of her plump, white thighs.

Reaching into his back pocket, he pulled out her panties and rubbed the silk against his cheek. She moaned and undulated her hips. "Show me your pussy, sweetheart."

Her skirt dropped back down around her body as her hands disappeared behind her back. Then she raised her hands back to her breasts, cupping and kneading them as she pushed the bustier lower, releasing them from the confining fabric. With her skirt unzipped, every sway of her body shifted it lower. First her belly-button was exposed, then her hipbones. Fuck, he'd never seen anything this erotic. With one final shimmy, the fabric fell to the table beneath her. Stepping away from the froth of material, she kicked it to one side.

The dark wood of the pool table gleamed in the dim lights. Like some sensual dream, she continued to move sinuously on the green felt top. Her hair was tousled and sexy, her eyes and part of her face covered by her black-and-red silk mask. The full lips that he longed to devour were parted. The bustier was still wrapped around her waist and torso but her breasts were totally exposed. Big and full and crowned with large, rosy tips that were puckered into tight buds, they were magnificent.

Her hips flared wide and her stomach had a gentle slope that invited his hand to trace the contours. Her long legs were covered in sexy, black fishnet stockings that exposed only her upper thighs. Her feet were arched in those tall heels that he found so sexy. What did women call them? Fuck-me shoes? Well, they were certainly working. He couldn't wait to fuck her.

But it was her pussy that drew his attention. The nest of hair at the apex of her thighs was the same lush color as her hair. Curly and soft, he wanted to run his fingers through it before parting her slick folds and sinking his fingers into her hot depths. As she moved to the music, he glimpsed the wetness on her thighs and pubic hair. She was hot and ready for him.

He didn't think it could get any more erotic than this. Then she bent over and picked up a cue stick.

FOUR

ELLY COULD BARELY KEEP her balance on the table. The way Liam was staring at her was making her legs weak. When he stared at her pussy and licked his lips, she almost dropped to the table, spread her legs and begged him to taste her. She'd probably do that too, but not yet.

Her inner core was pulsing in time to the music as one song ended and another began. She felt totally unlike her normal self. She felt sexy, self-assured and very erotic. Like some exotic creature, she could do things the normal Kelly wouldn't even dream of. With that in mind, she bent over and picked up a cue stick that had been pushed against the side of the table.

Straightening, she stepped to the edge closest to Liam. Planting the stick firmly on the table, she fitted the front of her body against it. Then, using the stick for support and leverage, she spread her feet wide, bent her knees and slowly slid the lower half of her body down the cue. It wasn't exactly a stripper's pole, but it was close enough.

Liam's eyes were glued to her pussy as she pulled herself back up. The smooth wood of the stick pressed against her swollen clit with every movement of her body. Cream flowed from her inner core as she repeated the motion several more times. Closing her eyes, she pushed her pussy harder against the wooden cue stick as she bent her knees again and began the slow journey down.

"Fuck." Her eyes popped open when Liam cursed. Still staring at her, he dragged his shirt over his head and dropped it to the floor. She could see the sheen of sweat on his chest, matting the light sprinkling of hair that spread from nipple to nipple before angling downward in a thin line and disappearing into the waistband of his pants.

But he wasn't finished. He practically tore the button off his jeans in his haste to open them. She discovered to her delight that he wasn't wearing any underwear when his cock sprang free from its confinement. Long and thick, the plum-shaped head was red from arousal. As she watched, fluid seeped from the slit. Wrapping his hand around the base, he held his erection and gave it one hard pump before releasing it.

Kelly decided it was time to make another one of her fantasies come true.

Falling to her knees, she discarded the cue stick. Pulling herself to the edge of the table, she swung her legs over the side. She pushed herself off the table and took the two steps necessary to bring her right in front of him. Then she began to move again.

Carefully, she twirled and stepped to his side. Leaning down, she rubbed one of her breasts against his arm as she blew in his ear. He reached out his hand but before he could touch her, she'd scooted behind him. Sinking her fingers into his scalp, she massaged the top of his head. Liam practically purred as she continued to run her fingers though the silky strands of his hair.

Shifting again, she flitted around to his other side, nipping at his neck and ears before moving on. Dancing her way back in front of him, she threw one leg over his lap and lowered herself onto his hard thighs. Then she did what she'd wanted to do for an entire year. Leaning forward, Kelly kissed him. Skimming her lips across his, she had her first taste of Liam—hot and masculine, with just the slightest taste of whiskey. Using her tongue, she traced first his top and then his bottom lip.

Liam's hand cupped her head, holding her steady as he plunged his tongue into her mouth. Taking his time, he explored and withdrew then forged into her mouth again. There was no part of her mouth that he didn't stroke or taste. Kelly had been kissed many times in her life, but never like this. This was a claiming on the most basic level.

Holding her still for his kiss with one hand, he brushed the tip of her breast with the other. Kelly shivered. "Tell me your name, mystery lady?" he whispered roughly.

For a moment, panic threatened to overwhelm her. No. There was no way he could find out who she was. There was no future for them and she didn't want to risk either their friendship or her job. Tears welled in her eyes and she started to pull away.

As if he sensed her turmoil, he began to soothe her immediately. "Shh, sweetheart. You don't have to tell me." He peppered her face with kisses as he cupped both her breasts with his hands and gently flicked the swollen nubs with his thumbs. His cock was rock-hard against her stomach as she pushed herself closer to him. "It's enough that you're here with me now."

His lips covered hers and all her worries were buried once more, replaced by the desire that always pulsed so close to the surface whenever she was around him. She had to give herself a mental shake to remind herself what she'd set out to do.

When he skimmed his fingers down her stomach toward her throbbing sex, she knew that if she didn't move now, she'd lose her only chance to do this. Putting both hands on his shoulders, she pushed herself back off his lap.

She sensed his surprise and then his pleasure as she lowered herself to her knees in front of him. Pushing his thighs wide with her hands, she scooted closer.

The long blue vein that ran the length of his erection seemed to pulse in time with the music. Her pussy clenched so hard, she gasped for breath. She ached so badly for his touch. But first, she wanted to take him into her mouth and taste him, lick him and suck him to completion.

Licking her lips, she leaned forward and ran her tongue along the entire length of his penis before swirling it around the head. Liquid continued to seep from the tip and she lapped at it daintily with her tongue. Liam groaned. "You're killing me, sweetheart."

Looking up at him, she smiled before lowering her head again. This time, she opened her mouth and sucked the head inside. His fingers clenched in her hair, allowing her no escape, but she had no intention of going anywhere.

Cupping his testicles in her hand, she carefully rolled them between her fingers. She was rewarded with another groan as he thrust his hips toward her, pushing his cock deeper into her mouth. She decided right then and there that she definitely liked this. Gripping the base of his erection with her other hand, she pumped her silk-clad fingers up and down as she devoured him greedily.

He used his hold on her to guide her rhythm. With each stroke, his cock went deeper. "I want to fuck that sweet mouth and then I'm going to fuck that hot, wet pussy." His words made her hum with desire as she continued to suck his cock as deep as she could take it. He was big, so it was difficult, but she opened her mouth as wide as she could. She wanted as much of him as she could get.

"That's it, sweetheart," he crooned. "You can take more." His hips were thrusting hard, his breathing harsh as she gently squeezed his testicles. He groaned and swore, his hips jerking as he came in her mouth.

Although she'd been expecting it, she wasn't quite prepared for the hot rush of semen in her throat. She gagged once then swallowed and continued to suck until she'd drained him. Finally, at his gentle urging, she released him and leaned her head against his leg. His fingers were still tangled in her hair but when they accidentally jostled her mask, she sat up quickly and fixed it.

Liam frowned and sighed but said nothing. Cupping her face in his hand, he traced her lips with his thumb. "Thank you."

"It was my pleasure," she informed him, nipping at the tip of his thumb before sucking it into her mouth.

Liam's low rumble of laughter vibrated though her. "Enough of that, sweetheart. Now it's my turn." Standing, he zipped his jeans again, just enough to keep them from falling.

Staring down at her, his eyes were filled with promise. "Come." He held out his hand and waited for her to take it. She trusted Liam implicitly and immediately slipped her hand into his. Lending her his strength, he helped her to stand. She was grateful for his arm around her waist when she swayed on her feet. "Just a few steps," he promised.

Turning her so that she was facing him, he placed his arms around her waist and lifted her onto the side of the pool table. "Lie back." She placed her hands on the surface behind her and lowered herself until her back was against the felt-covered top.

Bending down, he wrapped his hands around her ankles and lifted them, placing them on the edge of the table. "Now, spread your legs wide."

Kelly slid her shoes along the smooth rim until her legs were as far apart as they would go. "Beautiful," he murmured as he snagged a chair and pulled it over. It aroused her to know that she was spread across the table for his pleasure and that he was seated in a chair just looking at her pussy.

"Now, I want you to keep your legs just like that." His hands were warm against her skin as he skimmed his palms up her thighs toward her sex. He positioned her hips so that her ass was perched right on the edge of the table. That spread her wide open right in front of him. She knew that she was soaked and could feel her juices dripping down her thighs but she didn't care.

His thumbs traced the folds of her pussy before spreading them. "So pink, so pretty and so fucking hot." He leaned forward until she could feel his breath on her. She cried out and thrashed her head. Her heels dug into the wooden rim, gouging deep as she struggled to keep her legs apart.

Her breasts ached so badly, she covered them with her hands.

Rolling her swollen nipples between her fingers, she pinched them tight, crying out again as she did so. Liam looked up from between her spread thighs and growled. "First I'm going to eat you and then I'm going to fuck you."

"God, yes." There was nothing else she could say.

FIVE

*L*IAM WAS IN AWE of the woman lying so open in front of him. She was incredible. She gave him everything he asked for, holding nothing back. Sprawled atop the pool table like some exotic sex slave, she was willing to fulfill his every desire. Although he'd come minutes before, his cock was already hard and eager to go again.

The only thing marring the encounter was her refusal to share her name but Liam shoved that thought aside. Right now, he had her right where he wanted her and he planned to enjoy it.

Her fingers were plucking hard at her distended nipples so he knew she was close to orgasm. It wouldn't take much to push her over the edge. That was fine with him—he knew she couldn't be too comfortable with the raised edge of the table digging into her lower back.

Returning his attention to the V of her thighs, he traced the pink folds of her sex with his finger. He marveled at how wet and ready she was for him. Her arousal teased his nostrils. She even smelled hot. Her clit was swollen, the hard nub poking out from behind its hood. He lightly brushed his finger over it. Her lips parted on a breathy cry as she arched her hips toward him.

Carefully, he inserted one finger inside her, testing to see just how tight she was. Her vaginal muscles clamped down hard, gripping his finger. She was so hot and damp. He knew she could take him.

Withdrawing, he watched her as he pushed two of his long, thick fingers into her heated depths. The sensitive muscles gave way to the pressure. Liam groaned, imagining his cock buried to the hilt within her. This time when he pulled his hand back, he kept the tips of his fingers just inside the entrance. Leaning forward, he flicked her clit with his tongue at the same moment he thrust his fingers back into her pussy.

She cried out and frantically began to pump her hips. Liam hooked his free arm under one of her thighs and lifted her leg over his shoulder before clamping his hand on top of her stomach to hold her steady. He sucked her slick folds and clit as he pumped his fingers in and out of her body.

Her chest was heaving as she struggled for breath. Her hands were no longer on her breasts. Now, her fingers were tangled in his hair, tugging him closer. She cried out, she moaned, she thrashed. No woman had ever responded so honestly and completely to his touch.

He felt the change in her and knew she was close. Pulling his mouth away, he blew on her heated flesh as he plunged his fingers deep. She screamed as she came. Her hips pumped wildly and he could feel her inner muscles clamping down hard on his fingers. His cock was throbbing in time to her pussy. Next time, he would be buried inside her.

When she finally collapsed back against the table, he carefully withdrew his hand. She flinched slightly and moaned as her fingers unclenched from his hair and her arms flopped back on the table beside her. Slowly, he lifted the leg that was draped across his shoulder and let it hang over the side of the table. Then he lowered her other leg. He smiled when he saw the deep gouge in the wooden rim of the pool table and traced his thumb over it. It would forever remind him of this night and of her.

Standing, he leaned over her as he reached down and released his cock from his jeans. He pushed his hips closer to her, his erection brushing against her pussy, stroking her clit. She moaned and shivered before opening her eyes. She stared up at him, a sleepy, sated smile on her face.

"You are so damn sexy." The words were out of his mouth before he knew he meant to say them, but they were true.

"Thank you." She closed her eyes and he was afraid if he left her there too long, she might drift off to sleep. That was fine, later. When they were finished down here, he planned on carrying her upstairs to his apartment and tucking her into his king-sized bed with him right beside her. But first, he wanted to take her against the pool table.

"Hey, sweetheart." He leaned over her, placed his hands on either side of her head and traced the seam of her mouth with his tongue. Her lips parted easily and he thrust his tongue inside. He tasted the slight tartness of the wine she'd drunk earlier mixed with the musky flavor of his semen. His cock flexed in anticipation.

She reached up and cupped his face as he kissed her. Her tongue stroked his and when he withdrew, she followed, sliding her tongue into his mouth. He angled his head, deepening the kiss, never wanting it to end. Her fingers gently caressed his face before sliding into his hair. He growled deep in his throat. She was so open and giving, holding nothing back.

Her body began to move beneath his, her hips undulating, searching for him. His fingers dug into the felt of the pool table as he plunged his tongue back into her soft, seductive mouth for one final taste. Liam flexed his hips slightly, the motion causing his shaft to slide over the sensitive flesh of her pussy. It wasn't long before her thighs were clamped around his sides, squeezing him tight.

He broke away from the kiss and brushed his hair out of his eyes, wanting to see her. They both were sweaty and sticky. She looked magnificent sprawled in front of him, her eyes half-closed and her lips parted and moist. Her breasts were damp with exertion and the smell of sex wafted up from between them.

Liam had high hopes he could convince her to take a shower with him later. He took her hands in his and stepped back, pulling her into a seated position. Gripping her waist with his hands, he lifted her off the side of the table. She teetered slightly on her heels but he kept one arm around her waist to steady her.

"I want to fuck you now." Her head jerked up as he spoke and he watched the play of emotions cross her face. He could see her blue eyes in this light and watched as the sensual haze cleared and understanding filled them.

"Oh, my. We haven't . . ." she lifted her hand and dropped it again as a small smile played around her lips. "Yet."

"No, not yet. But I want to if you're up to it." As much as it would kill him, if she was too tired, he'd carry her upstairs and tuck her into his big bed before curling up behind her. She was so tall, she'd fit him perfectly.

"I definitely want to." Her words were more of a purr as she walked her nimble fingers across his chest and flicked his flat nipples.

"Good." He turned her around to face the table before she had a chance to do anything else. Much more of those roving fingers and he'd come too quickly.

"Hey," she objected, looking back over her shoulder.

Liam gripped her hips in his hands and tugged her back toward him. "I want to take you from behind, sweetheart. I want to hear the slap of my flesh against yours. You're tall enough and filled out enough that I don't have to hold myself back."

She frowned at him. "You mean I'm big and fat."

He was appalled at her interpretation of his words. "Who the hell called you fat? You're absolutely perfect." He allowed his hands to roam over her hips before cupping her ass. "You're a real woman with curves to entice a man, to cradle him as he fucks you. With you, I can let myself go and enjoy myself, knowing that I'm bringing you pleasure as well. Do you have any idea what a gift you are?"

She blinked at him, appearing dubious.

He clamped an arm around her waist and pressed his erection against her ass. "Does that feel like I'm lying?" She wiggled her behind and he shuddered. Damn, he was close. "Sweetheart. I need you now."

"Okay," she said, turning her head back toward the table. "What do you want me to do?"

Liam's gut clenched tight. "Bend forward and place your hands against the edge of the table." He kept his arm around her waist as she bent over. Her fingers gripped the rim tight. "Now, spread your legs." Inserting his booted foot between her legs, he nudged them apart. She widened her stance.

Stepping away from her, he admired the pretty picture she made. Her breasts swung free with the bustier still wrapped around her torso. Naked from the waist down, except for her stockings and shoes, she was just begging to be fucked. Oh yeah. She was perfect. Almost.

His hand descended smartly against one fleshy globe of her ass. The smack was loud in the room and Liam realized that, somewhere along the way, the music had stopped. She jerked and gasped but didn't move. He did the same to the other side of her ass, satisfied when both cheeks flushed pink. Covering them with his hands, he gave a squeeze. "The smacks don't really hurt but they bring the blood to that area. Your ass and your pussy will be even more sensitive now."

"Do it again."

He blinked, not sure he'd heard her correctly, but she moaned and pushed her bottom back against him. Stepping back, he smacked her twice more—sharp smacks that stung more than hurt. He ruthlessly controlled his strength. He'd cut off his hand before he'd truly hurt her. This was different. This was a lover's game.

But enough was enough. Her ass was pink, her pussy was wet and his cock was screaming for release. Reaching into his pants pocket, he pulled out the condom he'd put there earlier in the evening. He tore the packet open, quickly sheathed himself and moved between her spread thighs. Positioning his erection so that just the head was inside her, he gripped her hips with his hands and surged forward, not stopping until he was buried to the hilt.

Groaning, he dropped his forehead against her back and struggled for control. With her vaginal muscles squeezing him tight, however, control was impossible to find. "I'm sorry, sweetheart." Gritting his teeth, he pulled his hips back before pushing them forward. Sweat rolled down his temple. Her inner muscles gripped him tight as he withdrew almost all the way before plunging deep again.

He was going to come. There was absolutely no way to stop it. His balls were drawn up tight against his body and he was two or three strokes away from completion. Reaching one hand around her, he found her clit with his fingers and stroked the sensitive bud, praying he could coax her into another orgasm before he exploded.

He pumped hard. Once. Twice. And then it was all over for him. His hips jerked as he emptied himself into the condom, cursing it even as he realized it was necessary. He'd wanted so badly to feel her, flesh against flesh, but even this felt unbelievably good. When he relaxed against her, he realized that she was still shaking and bucking against him. Her body was wracked with spasms as her own release shot through her. Her vaginal muscles contracted around his cock, making him groan. Damn, she felt fantastic. Eventually, the spasms lessened and finally stopped and she gave a soft sigh as she relaxed.

Liam wasn't sure how long they lay slumped against the pool table but he knew he had to move. Carefully, he withdrew his cock from her. She crumpled, legs giving out from beneath her.

He caught her in his arms and carried her over to a chair, gently depositing her there. Brushing her hair away from her forehead, he smiled down at her. "I'll be back as soon as I get cleaned up. Then we'll talk."

He whistled all the way to the men's room.

SIX

KELLY WATCHED LIAM WALK away, mesmerized by the play of muscles in his back. She really would have liked to see his naked butt but he'd tugged up his jeans again. Once he was out of sight, it occurred to her that she was sprawled quite inelegantly in a chair.

Forcing herself to sit up, she looked down at herself. Mostly naked, she looked totally debauched. She smelled of sex and sweat and felt very sticky. The things they'd done made her want to bury her face in her hands and blush, but when they'd been doing them, they'd felt absolutely right. She had no idea how she was going to face Liam tomorrow. The only reason she wasn't in a total panic was that he had no idea who she really was. But he would soon demand answers.

That thought galvanized her into action. Surging to her feet, she hurried over to the pool table and plucked her skirt off the floor. Shaking out the layers of fabric, she stepped into the skirt and quickly zipped and buttoned it. She didn't think it was possible for her to run in heels but she did so now, quickly racing back to the bar. Yanking up the ends of the bustier, she shoved her breasts back inside. Grabbing her coat, she ran for the door. She didn't look back, afraid if she did, she wouldn't be able to leave.

She was almost to the door when she heard the pounding of boots behind her. Fumbling for the locks, she almost had the door open when his large hand slammed against the door with a bang. Kelly jumped but refused to turn around.

"Going somewhere?" The tone of his voice suggested that he was mildly interested in her reply but Kelly knew the truth. Liam was furious.

"It's time for me to go home." She felt his hands on her shoulders and she hunched forward. He sighed and withdrew. She missed his touch the moment it was gone.

"So you were just going to run out and never tell me your name." Kelly forced herself to turn around and face him. He looked hurt and angry.

Gently, she cupped his face in her hand. "I never meant to hurt you."

"Then what did you mean to do?" She could tell by the look in his eyes that he honestly wanted to know.

"I wanted to fulfill a fantasy."

"And this was the only way you could do it?" His voice was softer now and his hand covered hers, holding it against his face.

Closing her eyes against the pain, she took a deep breath and opened them again. "Yes. Disguised in a costume, I can masquerade as something I'm really not."

"And what's that?" Liam rested his other hand against the small of her back, subtly urging her closer.

"A sexy, desirable woman who can seduce the man of her dreams."

He frowned at her. "You are sexy and desirable."

Kelly shook her head. "It's just the costume, the masquerade, this special night. In the light of day, I'm ordinary and plain. Just like the decorations." Lifting a hand, she motioned to the room. "They looked so fantastic tonight but when your staff comes in to clean up tomorrow morning, they'll just look tacky and worn."

"So what we just shared wasn't special?" His words were laced with anger and what she thought might be pain. This wasn't supposed to happen. She only wanted to grab one night of happiness for herself, not hurt him.

"No." She shook her head in denial. "What we shared was more special than you'll ever possibly know. But it's not real. It's only for this one night." Drawing on every ounce of strength she possessed, she pulled away, both thankful and hurt when he just dropped his arms and let her go.

She gave him a shaky smile and turned back to the door. She had the locks undone and her fingers wrapped around the handle when he spoke. "You really think I didn't know it was you, Kelly?"

Her suddenly nerveless fingers fell from the door as she turned back toward him. With his arms crossed over his chest, his legs spread wide and his long hair tousled, he looked more like a pirate than ever. "How did you know? How could you know?"

"How?" He leaned toward her, crowding her back against the door before placing a hand on either side of her head, effectively caging her within his arms. "I've been watching you for a year now, sweetheart."

She shook her head, unable to believe his words.

"Oh yes," he continued. "I know every curve of your luscious body. I know that you laugh at the customers' stupid jokes and that you're kind to everyone you meet, without exception. I know you love baseball but hate football." He gave her a loving smile. "That's a serious flaw but I can overlook that." His dark eyes continued to search her face. "I know your favorite perfume is some exotic, flowery concoction that's both subtle and wild at the same time and that it makes my cock throb. You have a weakness for expensive dark chocolate. I know you prefer white wine to red and that you'd rather stay home and curl up with a good book or a movie than party all night long."

Her head was spinning but he wasn't finished yet. "I know that I've wanted you from the moment you came to work for me but you were an employee and I never get involved with my staff. If you'd ever shown a bit of interest in me, I'd have been tempted to fire you just so I could fuck you. But you never gave me any encouragement and you're too damned good a friend and waitress to lose."

"I didn't know." Kelly knew that Liam would never have fired her because of his attraction but that it was his way of letting her know just how badly he wanted her. It was strange to have her perceptions changed so quickly. Had she been wearing blinders for the past year or was he as good at hiding his feelings as she was? No matter, the truth was out now and there was no going back. She tentatively placed her hand on his chest, almost afraid to touch him now. She could feel the heavy thud of his heart against her palm.

"Of course you didn't know. I wasn't going to jump you in a back room if you weren't interested. And it's obvious you have no idea just how damn sexy you are even when you're wearing your hair pulled back tight with your white blouse buttoned to your chin."

Kelly could hardly keep up with Liam. "You think I'm sexy?"

"You are walking, talking sex." He smiled at her. "All those buttons just make a man want to unbutton them and discover the treasures you keep hidden underneath." His smile died. "I've bared my soul. What about you? How do you feel?"

"Oh, Liam." She flung her arms around his waist and buried her face against his chest. "I've wanted you from the moment I saw you and I've loved you for months. I just could never imagine that you'd feel the same way."

She felt him stiffen the second the word "love" came from her mouth but it was too late to call it back now. It was time to lay all her cards on the table. Leaning back against the door, she stared him straight in the eyes. "I love you, Liam Brannigan. What do you have to say about that?"

His face gave no indication of his emotions and he paused for so long that Kelly began to worry. But then a slow smile covered his face. "I'd say that I'm a very lucky man." He brushed her cheek with his fingers. "And that I love you too."

Reaching up, he hooked his fingers in the strap of her mask, slowly lifting it from her face. "It's time to unmask the mystery lady to reveal the woman I love and want in my life."

Kelly blinked up at him, glad to finally have the hot mask off her face. She wasn't afraid to face him any longer, knowing that he saw her as she truly was and loved her for it. Liam swept her up into his arms and swung her around in a circle. Laughing, she gripped his neck tight for support. When he finally stopped, her head was still spinning but she was smiling.

"Lock the door again, sweetheart." Liam held her next to the door while she turned all the locks. With her still in his arms, he carried her from table to table around the room until the few remaining candles that hadn't burned themselves out were extinguished. Then he headed toward the set of stairs that led to his apartment.

Kelly toyed with a lock of his hair. "So," she began. "Does this mean I'm fired?"

He was halfway up the stairs before he answered her. "Well, it does pose a problem. But you're too good a waitress to lose. All the customers love you." When he gained the top of the stairs, he walked toward his apartment door and opened it. Stepping inside, he shut it with his hip and leaned against it. "I guess I only have one solution."

"What's that?" His blue eyes held a warmth that curled her toes.

"I guess you'll just have to marry me."

Kelly smiled up at him, knowing he'd just offered her everything she'd ever wanted. "I guess I will."

He carried her down the hall and into the master bedroom, kicking the door closed behind him.

VELVET STROKES

SUSIE CHARLES

ONE

"WHAT'LL YOU HAVE TO drink, sunshine?"

Though the cavernous room was dark, Tom's head pounded in time with the flashing beat of the multicolored strobe lights. Blue, red, green—the pulsing colors shot like steel skewers through his blinking eyes. What had begun as a minor twinge over his right temple when he left his loft had developed into a full-blown, clenching vise of a headache by the time he reached the center of London.

He spun slowly to face the deep, male voice barking in his ear over the discordant thump of the most God-awful music he'd heard in years.

"Are you addressing me?"

"No, I'm speaking to the leprechaun on your shoulder, mate. What'll it be?"

A quick glance at the top shelf gave him enough information to realize that even purchasing a half-decent scotch was highly unlikely.

"Thanks, but I'll pass."

"Well then, if you're not drinking, or even thinking about drinking, move away from the bar."

"Why?" Moving away from the bar would require him to mingle in the sweating, heaving mass of humanity currently gyrating a few feet from the dubious but relative safety of the bar area. He'd come with one task in mind, and getting his body rubbed by some deviant with enough body piercings to pop rivet the Titanic, or have his butt pinched by a leather-clad Lothario in the mostly gay bar was not on his agenda—anywhere.

"Because you're standing there frowning, with a stick stuck up your cute, aristocratic ass, and you're scaring away the customers. That's why. So drink up, or shift it. *Capisce?*"

He gritted his teeth, struggling to maintain his calm under such direct provocation. "I'm here to see Elizabeth."

"Elizabeth who?"

"Elizabeth Burnett," he yelled, trying to make himself heard over the nonsensical, hyped-up jabbering of the DJ. "The owner?"

"Oh, you mean *Lizzy?*"

His lips firmed as he nodded.

"Yeah, well take a load off, sunshine. *Away* from the bar." He tossed his head in the direction of an outbreak of yahooing and catcalling ten feet away. "Your *Elizabeth* is gonna be a bit busy for a while by the looks of it."

Tom turned in the direction of the bartender's smug grin.

A stunning woman with long sable locks, wearing, from what he could ascertain, little more than a hot-pink satin bikini with a handkerchief masquerading as a skirt wrapped around her hips, was being hoisted, laughing, by four hulking brutes with shaved heads. Among the four of them they had enough tattoos, chains, piercings and leather to keep a fetish shop in business for a few months at least. Particularly disconcerting was the short but swarthy one dressed in little more than a leather jockstrap with suspenders going over his shoulders.

The crowd parted before them then surged back like a wave to fill in the gap created by their passing as they carried their precious, giggling cargo in the direction of the stage.

Music suddenly boomed from the speakers around the room. Some banal dance number had the many speakers—and his eardrums—vibrating and crackling from the intensity of the decibel output. At the risk of permanent damage to his cochlear faculties, he watched in appalled fascination as the woman and her overgrown quartet of captors began a libidinous display of dancing that would do a pole dancer proud. Oblivious to the hooting, lewd encouragement from the crowd, his attention fixed solely on the lady.

Elizabeth.

Two years and she hadn't changed.

Full, heavy breasts scarcely contained in the shimmering, straining triangles of pink satin. Glistening skin highlighting a slender waist that flared into an incredibly feminine set of wide hips. Barely concealed by a silky swathe of fabric that made his mouth water as he recalled running his tongue over every inch of exposed flesh.

His groin tightened.

Arms over her head, a smile creasing her beautiful face, she shimmied between two men touching and stroking her, who looked like they could devour her on the spot.

His anger flared. How could she let them paw her like that? It was indecent.

Shameless.

Wanton.

Absolutely and totally erotic.

And it should have been for his eyes only.

The music, the crowd, the flashing lights faded away as he watched her, spellbound. Another night. Another place. Lit by candles, sultry music floating around them as he lay back on the cushions scattered on the floor in front of his fireplace. Watching as Elizabeth danced, just for him. Her eyes holding his captive as she discarded piece after piece of clothing until she swayed in front of him in time to the haunting beat, naked . . . beautiful, the lush curves and sensuous essence a work of art he could never truly capture . . .

But it wasn't just for him any longer.

The truth of that slammed into him as the present came rushing back in to dispel the memory.

In spite of the disapproving grunt from the bartender, he rested his back against the bar, folded his arms, and prepared to wait for as long as it took.

Five minutes . . .

Ten passed.

Fifteen . . .

God, were they going through the whole damn song list? He couldn't watch anymore. Jealousy sat heavy in his gut, a raw burn of possessiveness that seared his insides.

"Where's the office?" he called out to the now occupied bartender.

"See that exit sign over there?" He jerked his head slightly behind him and to the right. "Down the hallway, past the toilets."

"Thank you," he replied abruptly and turned.

"I'd be careful though, if I were you."

Tom paused mid-stride and turned back to the mocking expression of the barman. "Dare I ask why?"

"We got some none-too-fussy clientele here who would just love to snuggle up to your sweet ass, sunshine." He laughed at his own joke.

Let anyone try . . . Tom was less than amused but bit back the retort that sprang to his lips. "Please inform Elizabeth that I'm waiting to speak with her," he said instead, and moved in the direction of the office.

As he strode down the dimly lit hallway, he savored the small amount of relief brought on by the muting of the raucously blaring music. He averted his eyes from the couple fondling and kissing in the small, darkened alcove just before the toilets, hurrying past in the direction of the "office" sign lit up at the end.

Thrusting his hands in his pockets, he leaned against the locked door and closed his eyes with relief, the pounding in his head abating slightly. In some detached part of his mind, he noted that the music had settled down, the catcalling had eased off. Hopefully that was a good sign . . .

"Now, aren't you a pretty one, sweetheart?"

Tom's eyes snapped open as a finger stroked down the side of his face. A Goliath of a man wearing an open leather vest and a studded leather biker cap, stood in front of him, smiling.

"I'm not your *sweetheart*," he gritted out, "and if you want to leave with all your body parts intact, I suggest you remove your finger, and get f—"

"Harry! You naughty thing."

A laughing feminine voice cut him off. But it was sufficient for "Harry" to step back and turn to her instead. The woman, her diminutive height dwarfed by the hulking hormone in front of her, stepped up to him without any fear and poked him in the chest.

"I've just left poor Nigel. He's been looking all over for you."

"Nigel? Is looking for me?" A huge grin broke over his face before he swooped her off her feet to plant a smacking kiss on her cheek. "That's music to my ears. Thanks, Lizzy luv. You're a darling." And strode off.

Elizabeth, her face sweat-streaked, her breath still a little uneven from her exertions, turned to face him, the smile slipping into a frown as she considered him. "It isn't a good idea to tell any of the guys around here to 'fuck off', Tom. It's a gay club—they tend to get a bit literal." She raised an eyebrow at him but didn't speak further as she unlocked the door and led the way into the office, softly lit by a row of recessed lights above the solid red cedar desk. Half a dozen security monitors showing various views of the dance floor and bar were inset into the wall on the right.

He moved into the middle of the room, taking in the professionally equipped space in contrast to the decadent bacchanal outside. In the sudden, blessed quiet, the sound of the door clicking shut behind him had him turning around.

Leaning back against the door, Elizabeth considered him, her startling cornflower blue eyes running down and then back up his body, a tight smile on her face.

"Since it's highly unlikely you've changed your sexual orientation, I can only assume you're slumming. Why is that? What would bring the great Thomas Danville down to my little den of iniquity?"

He shrugged, as if the sight of her standing there practically naked had no effect on him. It did though. And was the reason he kept his hands in his pockets, fighting the urge to reach out to her. He knew it would be less than well received. "A proposition."

"Oh, well this should be interesting." She didn't move from her spot, leaning against her hands on the door. He could only dream that she fought the same need to touch him. Dream was right . . .

"Is this what you wanted, Elizabeth? This . . . this life?" He glanced at the monitors.

"What do you mean 'this life'? I run a very successful club, Tom. 'This life' as you put it, has been good to me."

"I can see. Surrounded by deviants. Letting them paw at you, putting their hands all over you. You left me for this?" One of his hands left its pocket to wave at the monitors.

After a brief flare, her eyes shuttered, going blank, emotionless. "It's *my* life, Tom. And, therefore, none of *your* business," she snapped and pushed off the door.

Glancing down, he noticed red finger marks on the pale, creamy flesh of her arms, her waist, and became infuriated, knowing where they had come from.

"You don't have to do this. I could have given you better, Elizabeth. I offered—"

A sharp, mocking laugh left her lips. "Offered me what? A position as your mistress? A nice, cozy little apartment where you could visit me when it suited you?"

"That's rubbish! It wasn't like that—"

She spun on her heel, no more than an arm's length away, and held up her hand, cutting him off, anger pouring off her in waves.

Her words though, when she spoke, were controlled, so cool as to be almost icy. "What is it you want, Tom? I have a club to run, in case you hadn't noticed."

Great, he was managing to alienate her without even trying. And that was the very last thing he wanted to do. "Fine. Let's get back to business then. I need you, Elizabeth. For a special job."

"Yes, well, I hardly expected it to be for anything else. Sorry, I don't do artist's modeling anymore. For you or anyone else."

She turned to walk away, but he grabbed her arm and turned her to face him, anger beginning to simmer in his head along with the headache that had returned with a vengeance.

"You were never just a model to me, Elizabeth." He eased his grip slightly but didn't release her, awareness of the warmth of the skin under his palms filtering through him. Soft too, the skin smooth and silky. "And you damn well know it."

"So true, I was the little bit of fluff you liked to amuse yourself with. The naughty little secret your family wasn't to know about."

"Elizabeth—"

"Look, Tom, whatever it is, I'm not—"

"No. Hear me out. Please. Just hear me out."

"Fine. You have two minutes. Talk fast."

"You recall the 'Aphrodisia'?" he asked.

THE "APHRODISIA"? AS IF she could ever forget. With one word he managed to shatter her calm. Buried pain from the past crept under her guard, the small stab going straight for her heart.

The series of three highly sensual paintings had been the start of "them"—a catalyst for two years of uncontrollable hunger and passion that fed his artistic genius but nearly consumed them both . . . that nearly destroyed her. The past two years, since it all fell apart that winter's day, had been spent picking up the pieces and trying to rebuild her life.

"As you know, the Blonheim Foundation holds the original series," he said. "They've commissioned another set, a companion to the first three."

In spite of the unaffected air she assumed, in her mind Elizabeth gasped. The Blonheim Foundation rarely, if ever, requested works done specifically for them. And they only took the best—their gallery was full of masters, old and new. Tom had taken her to watch as "Aphrodisia" was mounted there, prior to the public viewing. For a specific request to come from them . . . She could understand what this meant to his career. It was on a par with a scientist being awarded the Nobel Prize. A pinnacle few achieved in their lifetime.

She glanced pointedly down at his hand on her arm until he dropped it. "Why me? Can't you find some other starving model to sit for you?"

"They want the original model. *I* want the original model, Elizabeth. I wouldn't do it without you."

She had to wonder why not, since, judging from reports in the press, he and his career seemed to have managed quite well without her—his *muse*—for the past two years. "How very touching. But as I said, I don't model anymore, Tom. No need. I'm a successful businesswoman now." She waved her arm at the office, the monitors, amazed at how easily the lie fell from her lips.

"Please consider it, Elizabeth. You'll be paid well."

Pain sliced through her and she turned away before he could

read it in her eyes. Why did it always come down to this, as if it was the crux of their relationship—he who had plenty and she who had none. "You never did get it, did you, Tom? For me it never was about the money."

God, how could he do this to her so easily? She inhaled deeply, bolstering her resolve. She'd known two years ago, in spite of the hurt, there would never be another man for her. Sometimes she wondered if the loneliness, the hunger for him that ate away at her would ever go away.

"Elizabeth . . ."

Strong hands caressed her shoulders, turning her back to face him. Looking into those dark, intent eyes, so close she could see the golden flecks in the iris, was like falling into the past, to a time when nothing mattered but the heat, the need, sating the unquenchable hunger that burned between them. She struggled against his grip.

"It was never, ever about the money, Elizabeth," he bit out in seeming exasperation, his tone gentling, "for either of us." Her heart stuttered as those hands slid up over the curve of her shoulders, her neck, to cup her face. Transfixed, her pulse skittering wildly, she watched as his head lowered, inch by inch, so close that his warm breath fluttered over her lips. "It was only ever . . . about this . . ."

A flicker of panic flared as she realized he was going to kiss her. Then it was lost, swamped under the feel of his warm lips closing over hers, his hands tilting her head so that the fit of their mouths was perfect. The achingly familiar caress that always left her yearning for more, crazy to touch him, taste him.

Her mouth opened on a gasp as his tongue licked, nudged.

Stealing between her parted lips as a groan rumbled up his chest and restraint was tossed aside as he thrust deep. His hands freed her head, slipping lower to wrap around her and pull her against him as he ate at her mouth with a fierceness that sent her senses reeling.

Hard. Everywhere her body touched his felt hot and hard. The noticeable bulge in his groin that made her clit throb with unfulfilled need as it pressed up against her, rubbing the ultrasensitive button as their hips rocked together in a familiar dance. Liquid heat flowed through her to dampen the flimsy barrier of her panties.

Tasting him. After so long without. With a muffled whimper, she sank into the kiss as though the intervening years had never been. And in a heartbeat, the memories she'd tried so hard to bury surged to the fore, supplanted by a new reality as her tongue curled around his, rubbed up against it in a primal form of mating that set her heart pounding and made her knees weak. The electric sensation that streaked through her from even that simple touch made her arch into him.

In a dizzying rush, her feet left the ground. Hands under her buttocks lifted her, the smooth wood of her desk cooling her flesh as she was perched on the edge. Strong male legs parting hers, stepping into the space formed as hers shifted, wrapping around his hips, his erection rubbing against her burning pussy.

So good. It felt so damned good.

Her hand moved down to grasp a tight buttock, pulling him closer. She needed more. Needed to feel him moving inside her, thrusting into her.

As if he shared her thoughts, the kiss deepened, became

wilder. His mouth ate at hers with a hunger she matched. Voracious. Insatiable.

All that mattered was his lips on hers. Her body aching for his, for the pleasure she knew could be found there. A pleasure she hadn't known in such a long time.

Moans filled the air—his, hers—she didn't know. She no longer cared.

Her pussy clenched, her clit tingling, preparing for the climax that built faster and faster. Close. The tremors building, her muscles tightening in anticipation.

Until a warm hand slipped under the scrap of silk covering her breast, rubbing the nipple between thumb and finger before pinching it, sending a small frisson of erotic pain arcing through her body directly to her throbbing clit. She gasped, the shock finally jolting her out of the sensual haze fogging her senses.

Even though her body screamed for release, she tore her mouth from his, slipping her hand from around his neck to push him away.

"No!"

Both of them were breathing roughly, Tom's heaving chest rising and falling as he sucked in deep draughts. He stared at her, his eyes dark, heavy, full of the same desire, the same thirst for more that she knew hers must mirror.

She wrenched her gaze away, down, traveling over his body, unable to stop her eyes from moving lower. His cock bulged and strained against the zipper of his designer slacks, a telltale dampness that could only have been from her staining the light gray front where their bodies had met.

Mortified, she considered what she must look like, seeing herself as he would—perched on the edge of her desk, hair disheveled, lips swollen, her legs splayed shamelessly. Part of her bikini top nudged to the side so that a reddened nipple was bared, the tip peaked in wanton display.

God, she must look like a whore.

And that was a little too close for comfort.

Tears gathered, but were tamped down with a deep shuddering breath as she tugged at her top to straighten it. The feeble attempt at restoring her modesty didn't help calm the emotions rioting through her body. The last couple of years of steeling herself against her body's response to this man, all destroyed with one kiss.

With as much dignity as she could muster, she closed her legs and slid off the desk. Her footing wasn't sure, her legs were like water, and she stumbled in the four-inch heels. Tom reached for her, but before he could touch her, she held up her hand.

"Don't . . . touch me." If he did, she'd be lost. All it ever took was one touch. "Please leave, Tom."

"Elizabeth. No."

Steeling herself, straightening her back, she looked up at him, unable to miss the raging lust—barely concealed by a look of concern—that still darkened his eyes.

"I can't do this, Tom. Not again."

"And if I promise not to touch you?"

Even now he looked like a tiger about to pounce, the tension on his face, through his body, indication enough that he was only just restraining himself. "You're kidding me, right? We haven't seen each other for two years, and in two minutes—*less*—look what happened."

His jawline firmed and he took a step back, thrusting his hands into his pockets as he dropped his head, breaking the connection of their eyes. "If you agree, we wouldn't be alone."

This time the pain shafted a little deeper, nipping at her soul. Of course. How naïve of her to think she, the muse, wouldn't have been replaced after all this time. "Oh, I see."

But as if he could read her mind, translate the straighter stance, the squaring of her shoulders, into what she was thinking, he reached for her, clutching her hand in a reassuring grip. "It's not what you're thinking, Elizabeth," he offered, and she caught the small flash of dismay in his eyes. "Do you honestly think I'd be so crass?"

"Well then, what?"

He let her hand go, turning away as if to consider his words. When he turned back to her, his expression was neutral, blank. "They've requested a couple this time—a woman and a man. An evolution of the original series."

Taking the half-dozen steps to her chair, she sank into it gratefully, before looking up at him. "And who did you have in mind?"

"Richard."

Her body softened in the chair, some of the tension draining away as a small, weak laugh broke free.

"Richard? That figures. Funny, he didn't mention it last week . . ."

"Where did you see Richard? And why?"

She looked up at the scowl in his voice, seeing a matching expression on his face.

"Richard and I meet for coffee or a drink every now and then.

Unlike some Danvilles," she flashed a brief, pointed look up at Tom, "he doesn't have a problem being seen with me in public. But then he never has much cared about what your family and friends think."

No, Richard was the black sheep of the Danville family, a role he relished. After spending ten years in an "acceptable" career in the SAS, he'd resigned his commission and nowadays spent most of his time freelancing as a fitness trainer. Ninety percent of his clients were female, which, she was sure, had a whole lot to do with him having a body that could tempt a saint to sin and a smile capable of melting half the polar ice cap when he turned on the charm. He was a six-foot-two stick of dynamite who had women falling over themselves for a chance to light his fuse. And though they'd kissed once or twice, succumbing to an attraction they both felt, for some reason they'd each pulled back, never taking it further. As if some invisible barrier stopped them.

She tapped her nail on the large blotter on her desk, her mind turning over. At least with Richard there, there'd be a buffer of sorts. "What would you need?" And why on earth was she even considering it? Curiosity? A perverse sense of masochism?

No, she knew why. In spite of what had happened between them, she had loved modeling for Tom. It allowed a sensual, decadent side of herself free, one that rarely saw the light of day lately, even in spite of her choice of occupation. It was the difference between business and pleasure. Not to mention knowing that she was someone's artistic inspiration had always been a heady thought.

"Two weeks. If you could get away from here. I need you full-time. You know how I work."

"How could I forget?"

When he was working, Tom was like a man possessed. Day or night lost all meaning—when the creative urge hit, he had to paint.

To think she'd lived that crazy life for the two years after she moved in with him. But then, she thought with a wrench, they'd mostly been happy days. Days filled with laughter, love, long nights when he wasn't working lying in each other's arms, gazing up through the skylight after making love. Or fucking on the rug, on kitchen counters, in the hallway . . . anywhere, anytime the urge took them . . .

She shook her head to shake off the memories as Tom spoke.

"I'd start with the preliminary sketches of you—Richard's are just about done—then you two together, working out the poses until I find the right three. Then I can get down to it."

His response was so brusque, so businesslike and unemotional, that she wondered if it would be possible after all. "I'll think about it. When would you need an answer?"

"Soon, Elizabeth. Blonheim's next exhibition is nine months away, and they want them for that."

Could she do it? Could she be around Tom and not want to touch him? Not want him to touch her?

His next words brought her back to earth with a thump.

"Since this is a purely business proposition, I'm offering you a quarter of what I'm being paid, Elizabeth. It will be very generous."

Money again. Well that took care of any delusions she might have had that he was trying to worm his way back into her life. But it was just as well, since with her current situation with the club and her finances, she could hardly afford to take a two-week "holiday".

"Naturally. But you realize I need to not only cover my own income, but also whoever I get in to manage things while I'm gone?"

"I said 'generous', Elizabeth. By that I mean it will be more than enough to pay off the loan you have on this place . . ." he looked around her office with a frown, the frown deepening when his gaze landed on the monitors, "and some left over besides."

A disconcerting thought started to work its way into her head. "And how do you know what I owe on this place?"

As she watched, waiting for his answer, he began to pace, not noticeably, but a random path around the office that allowed him to look anywhere but at her.

"The family has a seat on the board at the bank, currently filled by yours truly. I asked them to pull the details for me."

"You did what?" She stood, pushing her chair back so abruptly that it scraped across the linoleum. Anger boiled up inside her.

He stopped his pacing and stared back, his expression shuttered. "I know you've been struggling to make the payments the past four months. Not to mention the nursing home for your mother must be just about crippling you. You need this, Elizabeth."

Damn him! He knew then, all of it. Knew just how bad things were and she hated him having that leverage. "I don't need your stinking charity—"

He leaned over the desk at her, staring her down.

"It's not bloody charity. I just did my homework. That was a lesson *you* taught me, if you remember."

Oh, she remembered. She plopped back down in her seat. After he'd been shafted a couple of times by less than reputable agents in the early days and his career was faltering due to the industry backlash that washed over him, she'd taken it upon herself to show him how to find out about those he did business with. But he was right. She was having trouble making the loan repayments. Her mother's private nursing home care was just about killing her financially.

"Elizabeth, please. I didn't come here to fight with you. I need you."

And as much as it galled her to admit it to herself, she needed what he was offering, if what he said was true. She considered for a moment longer. Somehow she'd just have to keep it together. Two weeks. Surely she could manage that? And Richard would be there, so it wasn't as if they'd be alone . . .

"Okay. But I want a contract. Everything legal, on paper. I can be there in a week. That will give me time to get things organized here."

"Sounds perfect," he said and gave her a tentative smile. "Deal?"

He held out his hand. After a short pause where she wondered if she'd really, finally, lost her mind, she took it, shaking it lightly.

"I'll see you in a week." He lifted her hand to his lips and kissed it, squeezing it once before letting go and turning for the door.

"And Tom?" He paused and half turned to face her. "This is

probably unnecessary, but I'll state it anyway. I want the guest room. I'm not moving back into your bed."

His half-smile dropped and a cryptic look took its place. He nodded. "Understood."

He left, closing the door softly behind him.

She let out her breath. Hell, what had she just gotten herself into?

TWO

*Y*OU'RE DOING WHAT?"

Elizabeth flinched as her sister's response rose a few decibels above comfort level following her announcement about the job for Tom.

"The man treats you like dirt, totally disses you so that his poor, precious family won't know he's been mixing it up with a lowly little barmaid, has a fling with some rich tart while he's meant to be with you, and you're going back for more?" Debbie's voice rose higher the angrier she became. "You're nuts! Totally bloody certifiable."

"You make it sound terrible. It wasn't *all* bad," glared Elizabeth, steeling herself against the venting she knew was coming. "And it wasn't a fling—it was only a date."

"A date? A flippin' date? Oh, right. I forgot. And he couldn't take you to hobnob with his rich society friends *why*? No, he had to take Lady Muck so *she* wouldn't embarrass him."

"He never said that, Deb! It was expected that he go with her. It was a family obligation he couldn't get out of. She was a second cousin, or something."

"And one his witch of a mother felt would be eminently suitable for the title of Lady Danville once *she's* pushing up daisies, I'll bet." Debbie shook her head. "I can't believe it. You're defending him. So you've forgotten the bit where he would only ever mention you to his family as his *model*, even though you'd been living together for two blasted years? God forbid they might think he was sullying his pecker with some little nobody. Hell, you loved him, Beth. He supposedly loved you."

"He did love me, Deb. In his way . . ." *Just not enough*, thought Elizabeth, looking away as she felt the tears welling.

"So why didn't he fight for you? You walked out and he just let you go. What kind of love—"

"He called, you know." She shot a quick look at Debbie, catching the surprise on her face. It was a fact Elizabeth hadn't shared with anybody, even her sister. But then she'd withdrawn at that time, using the setting up of the club as an excuse not to have to answer questions or face what had gone wrong. "Many times . . . just after . . ." Her words petered out as she recalled the desolation in his voice, slowly replaced by the brief, curt, almost resigned tone, the calls coming further apart before they finally stopped altogether.

"And?"

"I wouldn't return his calls. What was the point?"

"Well, it still doesn't make it right. Dammit, he hurt you!"

"I appreciate your concern, Deb. But I'm older now. Wiser. Stronger. And this time it's purely business."

"Oh, really?" Her sister's tone was laced with disbelief.

"He knows about Mom. He knows I've been having trouble making the loan repayments on the club."

"How? Is he having you investigated?"

"He's on the board at the bank, Deb. Plus, he's a Danville. Anything is possible. But darn it, I'm so close. Only six more payments and the last two years of struggling and scrimping will be behind me. As it is now, I stand to lose the lot. I'm on a limited extension already—three weeks left to catch up on the three payments I owe, plus the next one, or they foreclose. And if that happens, then what? Go back to being a barmaid? Long hours, on my feet all night, six nights a week for barely a subsistence income?" She hung her head in her hands. "Can't you see what this job would mean? I'd own the club. Mom's care would be taken care of."

"Oh, sweetie, I'm sorry." Debbie looked contrite. "I had no idea things were so bad. And I'm so sorry Jase and I can't help you out financially with Mom. But we're barely breaking even ourselves. Some months not even that. If we couldn't live here, rent-free . . . God, what a mess."

She held her sister's hand and squeezed it reassuringly. "I know, Deb. It's just the way things are. But at least you visit Mom regularly, make sure she's okay. Hell, I feel so bad that I never see her, but I'm either sleeping or working."

"Come on, Beth, don't be so hard on yourself. Visiting Mom is the least I can do to help. If you weren't paying for her care, she'd be stuck in a public home . . ."

They shared a glance. They'd both heard horror stories of patients relegated to the public nursing homes. It just wasn't an alternative either of them could contemplate.

Elizabeth stood, walking over to the wide bay window, pulling aside the lacy curtain to catch the struggling winter rays barely melting the frost off the ground. She let the curtain drop and turned back to her sister. "But you understand why I can't pass up this opportunity, don't you? I received the contracts from his solicitor today. Tom's being more than generous. Much more. It's like he said—the amount will pay out the rest of the loan, go a long way to covering the nursing home expenses, and still give me a small nest egg. And it's only two weeks."

"And once you've paid off the club, then what? Honey, you're not getting any younger. Don't you want to find someone nice to settle down with? You're hardly likely to find anyone at your place. I mean, let's face it, they're lovely guys, most of them, but you aren't exactly equipped to ring their chimes, if you know what I mean."

Elizabeth shrugged. "It's a living."

The phone rang in the kitchen and Debbie excused herself to answer it.

Flopping back in the thickly cushioned old sofa chair—one that Jase had saved from being tossed out at an estate sale he'd attended for his and Debbie's fledgling business, and then lovingly restored—Elizabeth took a long sip of her coffee as she looked around. Their old home. In spite of the differences her sister's deft decorating touch had made, it was still home. The one place on earth she felt like her old self. It was cozy, comfortable. Certainly a lot more homey than her Spartan apartment above the club. That was somewhere to put her head down at night and little more. But it brought Debbie's comment back to her.

Her sister was more right than she knew, and certainly more so than Elizabeth would let on. After two years, she was tired of the endless round of working afternoons and long nights. Crawling into a lonely bed in the wee hours of the morning. Sleeping until lunchtime. Then the same routine again. Day after day. Night after night. How the heck was she supposed to meet anyone?

Apart from her immediate financial concerns, it was a big part of why she'd accepted Tom's offer. A way off the crazy merry-go-round that never seemed to stop. Maybe when she'd paid off the loan, she could sell the club and make a reasonable profit. It was one of London's most popular clubs for the gay community, after all. And even after putting enough money aside to pay for her mother's nursing home for twelve months, there might be enough to just take off for a while. Move. Live somewhere else where nobody knew her. Perhaps even start over. *Doing what?* she wondered.

She closed her eyes and leaned back, savoring the brief respite before she had to leave for the club.

"That was Jase. The delivery from that last estate auction has been held up in traffic, so he'll be late home." Debbie sat down opposite her again, perched on the edge of the sofa. "So when do you leave to do your Lady Godiva thing?"

"In three days. Just enough time to finish showing Graham the ropes so that he can hold the fort while I'm gone. He should be okay, though—he's worked at the club since before I bought it, so there isn't much that happens there he doesn't know."

"Well, don't worry about Mom while you're gone. I'll tell her you love her—even if she can't even remember me most of the time. But promise to call me, Beth. Any time—day or night—if you need to talk. Okay?"

"Thanks, Debbie. I will."

Debbie slipped her glasses down her nose and smirked as she peered over the top of them. "And keep your hands off hottie Richard. The sight of that boy's naked tush would give a Carmelite nun an orgasm."

"Deb!" laughed Elizabeth, relieved the mood had lightened. "You told me you didn't sleep with him." It had been three years since Debbie and Richard had dated a few times, before he'd had to leave for active service in Iraq. By the time he returned, Jase had moved in. Strange how things worked . . . it was actually through that association she and Tom had met the first time.

"I didn't. More's the pity. We did get naked, though." Her expression became distant, a goofy smile tilting up her lips.

With a mischievous grin, Elizabeth grabbed a tissue and reached over to her sister.

"What are you doing?" At the feel of the tissue, Debbie batted Elizabeth's hand away from her face.

Motioning with the tissue-wrapped finger, Elizabeth pointed in the direction of her sister's chin. "Sorry, sis. It's just . . . the drool. I thought I'd catch it before it ran off your chin."

Debbie scowled and brushed absently at her mouth. "Oh, har, har. Don't be ridiculous. Anyway, that was years ago. Richard's probably all saggy now."

Elizabeth shook her head. "Ah, nope. Not saggy. Far from it, actually. About as far as it's possible to get . . ." Elizabeth sighed and covered her smug grin with her coffee mug.

"And how would you know, missy?"

"We see each other now and then." Elizabeth smiled at Debbie's drop-jaw look. "And boy, oh boy, what that man can do to a pair of jeans . . . or for that matter, leather . . ." She sighed dra-

matically, earning her a thwack on the knee with a folded news-
paper from her sister.

"Bitch!"

She batted her eyelashes innocently at her sister. "But you
have Jase, Deb. He looks pretty good in denim too . . ."

"True." Debbie nodded, and sat back, a wicked smile creeping
across her face, her eyes twinkling. "Actually he looks *much* better
out of it."

Elizabeth rolled her eyes and held up her hand. "Okay.
Enough. TMI." Elizabeth put her cup down and stood. "I would
like to be able to look my brother-in-law in the face in the future
without blushing, thank you very much. Anyway, I need to get
going. I'll call you before I leave town." She leaned down to kiss
her sister's cheek.

"And during," reminded Debbie. "I want to know you're all
right. Or I'll just have to come up there and make certain for myself."

"Sure, sure. You're just looking for an excuse to catch another
look at Richard in the buff."

"Not true!" cried Debbie indignantly. At Elizabeth's raised
eyebrow, she blushed and grinned. "Well, maybe just a little
look . . ."

"Sit still, Richard! Christ, you're worse than a two-year-old."
Tom sighed in resignation and put down his sketchpad and pencil. "Ah, what the hell, let's take a break."

"About bloody time." Forsaking his reclining pose on the vel-
vet-covered antique chaise lounge, Richard swung his legs over

the side and stood, stretching, feeling the knots in his spine from maintaining the pose for so long pop and release. He moaned his relief. "Nice couch, by the way. Where the heck did you find it?"

"Would you believe Aunt Hermione's attic? I asked her if I could borrow it for a bit."

Richard's eyes widened and he choked down a laugh. "And you didn't tell her to what purpose it would be put, naturally."

Tom snorted. "No. Definitely not."

"I daresay this will be the first time in its illustrious history it's cradled naked bodies."

"It's been in Hermione's family for generations." Tom turned a wry look on Richard. "You need ask?"

"And now it will be the scene of my greatest moment." Richard gave a hearty sigh, hand clutched at his heart. "Elizabeth and me. Naked and frolicking on the crushed velvet, oblivious to the pained exclamations of the 'Creative One' as he implores us to 'hold that pose'. Oh, be still my beating heart!"

Tom laughed. "Give it up, you wanker." He picked up his sketchpad and pencil, preparing to put them on his desk, when he paused and turned. "By the way . . . how long have you been seeing Elizabeth?" He swiped Richard's jeans off the floor and tossed them to him.

"Since you two split up." Richard hopped on one leg then the other as he stepped into his jeans and pulled them up. "Why? Jealous?" He snapped the stud closed, watching Tom closely under his lashes.

"Don't be ridiculous."

"Of course. How silly of me." Still observing Tom discreetly while he pulled his T-shirt over his head, he noticed the pensive look on his cousin's face. But rather than ask, he waited, knowing his naturally reticent cousin would spit out whatever was on his mind—eventually.

Tom straightened the pencils, lining them up in a row, so that all the ends were level, fussing until they were perfectly even—a nervous trait of his cousin's Richard was very familiar with. "So what do you two talk about?" asked Tom.

"Oh, just . . . stuff. You know, her work, my work, my family, my love life . . . her love life . . ." Behind Tom's back he grinned at the rigidity that entered his cousin's tall frame at that. "You know. Stuff."

No way was he letting Tom off easily this time. The damn fool had lost the best thing in his life when he let Elizabeth go. It was about time he realized it.

"Does she ever . . . mention me?"

Bingo!

"In what way?" he asked innocently.

Tom headed toward the kitchen. Richard snagged his boots and socks and followed him.

"Never mind. It doesn't matter, anyway. It's better left as is."

Good God, the man was a bloody moron.

"You're a smart man, Tom. Smarter than I'll ever be. But when it comes to women, and Elizabeth in particular, you suck."

Tom put down the beer he was pouring and glared at Richard, anger flaring in his eyes. "What the hell do you mean by that?"

Richard grabbed the glass of beer, took a long gulp and sighed, feeling the chill all the way down. "If you need to ask, then my man, you do need help. Seriously."

"Might I remind you that *she* left *me?*"

"Oh, I remember. That and a whole lot more, and you fucked up. And like everything you do, you did a damn good job of it. I'll bet you haven't even figured out the reason she left you, have you?"

"She told me she didn't want to model anymore. She wanted a 'normal' life." He scowled as he resumed filling the second glass and took a long drink. "Right. So she buys a rundown club in Earl's Court and becomes the unofficial queen—no pun intended—of the gay club scene. How blasted 'normal' is that?"

Richard shook his head in exasperation, and made a noise like a buzzer on a game show. "Wrrrrrroong. As I said, you suck." He could hardly miss his cousin's perplexed frown. "Look. Think about those days, Tom. From Elizabeth's side, this time. Because you're missing the most important part." He rolled his eyes at the look of confusion on his cousin's face. "Here's a clue. Think back to what directly preceded Elizabeth leaving that day. Remember, you had a couple of visitors. Family, to be precise." Richard curled his lip in distaste. He'd been unfortunate enough to call in himself and caught the tail end of his aunt's visit. The interfering old biddy. "By the way, how is Aunt Caroline? Still trying to fix you up with half the eligible socialites in London?" When Tom continued to look at him blankly, he shook his head and reached down for his leather jacket, slipping his arms inside before braving the early winter chill outside. "Just think about it, Tom. All the answers you seek are right there—you just have to look hard enough." He glanced at his watch and cursed softly, tossing back the rest of his beer. "Look, I have to go. Got a date with a little lady I really don't want to keep waiting. She's hot for my gorgeous bod, you know?" He winked at Tom.

Tom turned a dry glance on him. "I've always felt your modesty was your best feature, actually."

Richard chuckled. "I'll be back in a week. Try not to piss off Elizabeth in the meantime. Be good and play nice."

THAT NIGHT, GLASS OF MERLOT in hand, Tom sat back on the sofa in front of the fire, staring into the flames as he mentally flicked back through the memories to those last days with Elizabeth. It wasn't a place he visited very often, mainly because of the pain that went with it. Never in his life had he felt as desolate, as devastated, as he did watching Elizabeth walk out that door. It was as if all the brightness, all the life was sucked out the door with her, and he was left with a dark, empty space.

The weeks that followed had been some of the bleakest of his life.

It was not a time he particularly wanted to revisit, but perhaps it was time. And if it held the key to losing Elizabeth . . .

Slouching down into a comfortable position, he straightened his legs out in front of him, cursing softly as his big toe kicked the leg of the coffee table. He looked down, his eyes resting not on his throbbing toe, but on the drawer underneath the coffee table that had been nudged open a crack. His lips firmed. Placing his wineglass on the table, he reached for the drawer, opening it to extract the heavy album that lay inside.

His fingers wandered over the hand-tooled leather cover of the photo album on his lap, tracing the indentations of the lettering. It had been one of Elizabeth's hobbies. Documenting their lives. His showings. His "great career." It had sat in the drawer under the glass-topped coffee table since the day she left. Not once had he looked at it.

The leather creaked, a slightly musty smell tickling his nose as he flipped open the cover.

Early days.

Shots of him in his studio—looking up with a paintbrush in his mouth, palette in hand, a startled look in his eye as Elizabeth caught him unawares. Or totally focused on whatever painting he'd been working on, oblivious even to her snapping him, a frown of concentration creasing his brow.

Family shots—Richard and him at Christmas at his parents', deep in conversation, glasses of wine in hand . . .

At his sister's wedding. His arm around his cousin Ann's shoulder. He chuckled as he recalled Richard taking the shot. The damn fool had backed up to get a better angle and had nearly fallen into the lake behind him . . .

The gallery opening for his "Insatiable" series. The shot with his mother and father he particularly recalled. Both of them standing stiffly beside him. While they supported his artistic endeavors, it was no secret, on his mother's part at least, that they wished he'd pursue something a little more "acceptable" than nudes, however artistically rendered. Landscapes, for instance.

He was halfway through the album before he found one of Elizabeth. He smiled fondly as the memory came back. Elizabeth had been posing for hours. He'd lost track of time, so absorbed as usual. Long after midnight, he realized she'd fallen asleep. Curled up on the floor like a kitten, the sheet she'd been draped in tucked up under her chin, she'd looked so beautiful, so innocent, he couldn't resist snapping her before he carried her to bed.

He flipped the page and found, it occurred to him with some consternation, one of the few photos of them together—her sister's wedding, this time. Elizabeth smiling as she looked up at him, his arms wrapped around her, the summer sunlight filtering through the weeping willow in the garden of the reception grounds kissing them with a mottled golden glow. He traced his finger over the photo, following the line of her hair as it tumbled down her back . . . When she'd looked at him like that, her eyes brimming with love, he would have done just about anything she asked of him.

Happy days.

The smile faded as a disconcerting realization began to filter in, casting a shadow over the happiness from those memories.

Page after page. Flipping further through the album, a sickening understanding settled over him.

It was the final photo of Elizabeth, though, less than a month before she left, he recalled, that hit him the hardest. He even remembered taking the damn photo. He'd spent an hour shooting her in preparation for a private commission. She'd been tired, he'd been frazzled because he couldn't get the pose and angle he wanted with the light just so, and had stomped away to get them both a coffee. When he returned, she'd been standing at the window, sheet wrapped around her, light angled onto her face, the expression exactly what he'd been trying to achieve all afternoon. In his excitement, he'd almost dropped the coffees in his rush to grab up the camera and capture it. What he hadn't realized, hadn't seen at the time, was that the sad look in her eyes hadn't been a pose. It was the look of someone who was truly hurting. But it was the unspoken plea in her blue eyes, the hurt and sadness he could only now read there, now that he opened his eyes fully and truly *saw*, that brought him undone.

His throat tightened. His eyes burned as the honest pain she'd been feeling back then hit him in the heart. Why hadn't he *seen* it? He was trained to pick up things others didn't. Could he really have been so blind to what was in her head . . . her heart?

He snapped the album shut and closed his eyes, willing away the dampness that had built behind his clenched lids as he breathed deeply, fighting the tightness in his chest.

The feeling passed, slowly, and he opened his eyes again, glancing down at the album before tucking it back into the drawer and pushing it closed with his foot. He tipped the last of the Merlot into his glass and held the ruby liquid up to the flame before upending the glass and swallowing the wine in one large gulp, feeling the quick burn as it raced down over the lump in his throat.

He let his mind wander. Fragments of memories, not just from that last day, but weeks and months before filtered in. Memories, seemingly unrelated at the time, but what amounted to a screwup of truly monumental proportions.

As a DOCUMENTARY OF THEIR life together, the album was a damning indictment against him as the world's biggest, most insensitive fool. Photos of him, of Elizabeth, even a few of them together, taken by other people—Richard, her sister, friends of Elizabeth's they'd visited. But never any of her with *his* family. At all the Danville family gatherings, not a single one. As if that was a part of his life—for two years—she hadn't been privy to. To his great shame, he couldn't even remember if he'd invited her to any of them. Where she'd gotten the photos from, he didn't know. Richard seemed most likely, since he was the only one of his family who knew of and understood his *real* relationship with Elizabeth. Mortification hit him hard at just how badly he'd treated her, to what extent he had taken her for granted.

In every way that mattered to a woman, he'd denied her. He'd never doubted that she loved him. She'd shown it every day, in what she said, what she did. How she looked after him so that he could concentrate on his art.

His fucking *art*. His lip curled with disgust.

Why had that been more important than giving back to the woman he loved half of what she gave him? He'd been driven back then. Obsessed. A budding, enthusiastic painter intent on rendering his visions of life as he saw it—his great, blasted masterpieces. Translating the beauty around him, the joy and love, the passion, but somehow missing the one thing, the one person who gave him that gift. Encouraged. Fostered it. The ability to see what others often missed, whose selfless gift of herself, her love . . . support, enabled him to unlock what he felt, saw, and bring a fraction of that passion to life under his brush.

But that final day . . .

His mother had arrived, unannounced as usual for one of her thankfully rare visits. Five minutes earlier and she would have found Elizabeth and him making love on the rug. As it was, he'd wandered out of the bathroom with a towel wrapped around his hips to find his mother interrogating a naked and very embarrassed Elizabeth.

That was bad enough, but he could hardly blame his mother

for what had occurred after she left. He flinched at the memory, Elizabeth's words from the club making perfect sense . . .

"Offered me what? A position as your mistress? A nice, cozy little apartment where you could visit me when it suited you?"

Stupid. He placed his now-empty glass on the table and held his head in his hands.

At the time it had seemed like the perfect solution—to him. Since he couldn't really move his studio, he'd had the brilliant idea to put Elizabeth up in an apartment nearby, close enough that he could spend the nights he wasn't working with her. Plus take her out of the line of fire of his mother's viperous tongue, and the rest of his family who disapproved of the "barmaid-model" who seemed to occupy so much of his time.

Instead of putting his damn obsession with his career, his paintings aside for however long it took, facing the whole bleeding lot of them and telling them he loved her and they could take the "good Danville name" and all go to hell, he had taken what he saw now was the easier path, thinking Elizabeth would understand. But he knew now she hadn't. And could he blame her? To make matters worse, if that was at all possible, he'd thought to sidestep the storm of disapproval, so they'd just leave him alone and let him get back to his precious painting, by introducing her—more than once—as his "model."

His fucking model!

But she'd never said a word. Giving him that line about wanting a "normal life." And after leaving a few messages on her answering machine, instead of chasing after her, he'd let her go, because *he* was hurt that *she'd* leave him.

Christ, he was a bastard. A stupid fucking bastard. How could he have done that to the woman he loved? No wonder she'd left. It was a miracle she'd even spoken to him the other night. He would have kicked his ass out the door before he got his mouth open.

But maybe, just maybe, he had one more chance with her. That kiss had been better than a memory. She still felt something for him. And this time, please God, this time, he'd make sure he did it right.

THREE

ITCHING HER BACKPACK A little higher to take the strain off her shoulders, Elizabeth slammed the boot shut on her old Beetle, glancing around the deserted parking lot next to the nondescript old brick warehouse with the fading paint.

"Sweet Lizzy Burnett. Well, I'd just about given up hope of seein' you here again, lass."

At the familiar voice, Elizabeth smiled broadly and turned toward the huge double doors, currently splayed wide open.

"Hello, Sara." She held her arms open for a hug from the tiny, gray-haired woman, inhaling the wonderful fragrance of Sara's signature lavender blend.

For years, Sara had rented a portion of the bottom floor of Tom's converted warehouse for her small aromatherapy business. She paid a pittance for the space, but Tom had always maintained he kept the rent minimal just because he loved the way she made the place smell, and she was a cheap guard for his private lift during the daylight hours. As far as Elizabeth knew, the only person who had a key to the building, apart from Tom and Sara, was

Richard. Anyone else had to run the gauntlet of the formidable lady in front or her.

Tom wasn't fooling anyone though—he really loved the old lady who treated him like a grandson. For Sara's seventieth birthday he'd presented her with a beautiful portrait of herself. Elizabeth remembered him working for weeks to get it just right. A lot of love had gone into that painting and it showed. And while it usually took a fair bit to render old Sara speechless, he'd managed it—she'd sputtered and stuttered until he picked her up and gave her a big hug.

So many wonderful memories, Elizabeth mused. "So, you haven't retired yet?" she teased Sara.

"And do what? Sit at home and watch the TV with our George? The man sleeps through more shows than he watches. Besides, the old dear is deaf as a post. The volume damn near blasts me out of me chair."

The air was richly laced with a surprisingly harmonious mix of spicy and floral scents. Elizabeth sniffed as she looked around. "I've missed this, Sara, walking in here and feeling as if I just tumbled into a wild country garden."

Sara stood back with her arms crossed and gave Elizabeth a considering look. "Well, you've been missed too, lass. And by more than me." Sara raised her eyes to the upper floor. "Hasn't been the same since you left. Damn near become a hermit." Then she brightened. "But now that you're back—"

"Oh no, Sara," Elizabeth interrupted. "You misunderstand. I'm only here for two weeks."

Sara's mouth firmed, her fists planted on her hips. "You're kiddin' me! Why, I've never seen two people more—"

Elizabeth kissed her cheek to stop the emotional outpouring of words, patting Sara's hand as she pulled back. "We two just weren't meant to be."

"Poppycock. And you know it. And so does his lordship up there." She jerked a thumb in the direction of Tom's loft. "Stupid man. But then they're all a bit daft. God didn't put women here to keep men company—it was so there'd be someone around with a brain and a bit of bleedin' common sense to run things."

Sara looked at her closely, gripping Elizabeth's hand firmly with both of hers. "Listen to an old woman, luv." Sara's voice gentled, the scratchiness of age apparent when she wasn't doing her usual shouting. "What you two shared isn't gifted to many—don't throw it away."

"It's too late—"

"Bah! It's never too late, lass. Not even when you're as old as me." Sara turned away and walked to her workbench. "Go on upstairs, lass. He's probably been pacing all morning waiting for you to get here."

"I'll see you later, Sara."

"Oh, you can count on it." Sara chuckled to herself, her shoulders shaking. "Just don't forget to invite me to the wedding," she tossed over her shoulder.

Elizabeth shook her head and couldn't resist a grin at the irrepressible old romantic. She pressed the button on the old lift. It slowly shuddered and groaned its way down to her, and she stepped inside, dragging the outer wrought-iron door closed, then turning the lever for the loft.

Memories hit her thick and fast as the lift rose. The familiar smell of turpentine and oil paints. The annoying creaking of the old service lift. Tom bringing her home from dinner at the small pub on the corner and taking her against the wall, ripping clothes open—his, hers—just enough to get skin to skin and his cock inside her, neither of them able to hold off the hunger and wait until they got upstairs . . .

Leaning her forehead against the wall, she closed her eyes and took a deep, shuddering breath. God, she had to stop. *It's just a job. It's just a job.* She repeated the mantra she'd been telling herself for the past week, whenever the memories started to creep in and overwhelm her.

As the lift slowed, she forced a smile on her face, mentally steeling herself for the impact of seeing him again.

Still, nothing could quite prepare her for the sight that greeted her when the lift stopped and the door opened into Tom's living room.

Tom. Paint-flecked jeans. Bare, muscled chest. A faint smile on his face and a palette in one hand as he held his other out to her. Damn.

"Hello, sweetheart. Welcome home."

FROM THE FLEETING FLICKER of sadness in Elizabeth's eyes as the words fell from his lips, Tom could have kicked himself. Shit! Richard was right—he truly sucked. But seeing her standing there, smiling at him, the sense of déjà vu had hit him right between the eyeballs, and the last two years had evaporated as if they'd never been.

"Sorry. I shouldn't . . . what I meant . . . I mean, what I was going to say . . ."

She stepped into the expansive room, brushing past him to wriggle her backpack off. He plonked his palette down on the console table and rushed to help her. The darn thing was nearly as big as she was, and she sighed and rotated her shoulders with relief when the weight was gone.

She turned to face him with a nervous smile. "Tom, it's all right." She looked around the foyer, the smile fading. "It does seem just like yesterday, doesn't it? And I know you didn't mean anything by it." Still, her gaze jumped around nervously while managing to avoid his face altogether, then her arms crossed over her chest so that she was almost hugging herself. She looked up at him. "The guest room's still the guest room?"

"Sure. Has its own bathroom now, too. So you can freshen up or . . . or whatever."

A cheeky but still nervous smile, a hint of the old Elizabeth, peeked out. "Oh, pooh! And there I had visions of stretching out in the Jacuzzi . . ."

So he wasn't the only one. Except he'd been indulging in memories of her in there with him every time he'd used it for the last two years. Naked. While he fucked her slowly, repeatedly, making her come again and again until she screamed his name and begged him to stop.

His cock stiffened in his jeans, pinching against the cold metal teeth of the zipper so that he flinched. His reassuring smile probably came out looking more like a grimace. "Well, if you want to. I mean . . . I meant . . ." He coughed in embarrassment. "God, I need to stop saying that. Look, if you want to use the tub, Elizabeth, feel free. Lock the door if it makes you feel better." He gritted his teeth and turned to walk away before he looked like a bigger idiot. A hand on his arm stopped him.

"Tom?"

He turned and looked at Elizabeth, surprised to see, not disgust or anger, but instead understanding. The hand on his arm gave a reassuring squeeze.

"This isn't going to be easy for either of us, Tom, I can see that. But this won't work if you keep worrying about what to say or what to do. So for the next two weeks, let's just try and be old friends. Sound okay to you?"

Old friends. Sure. Maybe. *Not*.

Still, it was better than nothing. Hell, he appreciated the fact that Elizabeth was being so generous, especially considering the way he'd treated her before. He covered her hand with his, feeling a slight tremble under his palm. "Sure, Elizabeth. And thanks."

"That's okay, I just want that tub later," she laughed, the sound still a little nervous. "Let me go unpack and take a shower for now. Then you can tell me what you want me to do."

She picked up her backpack and spun away before he could say a word. Just as well. He doubted she'd like to hear what he *really* wanted her to do.

Naked.

On the couch.

No, on his lap on the couch.

On his cock on his lap on the couch.

He closed his eyes and groaned, gripping the edge of the table.

Her sliding up and down, eyes locked with his as he cupped

her breasts and made love to her slowly, relishing every second of being inside her. Her juices running down his straining cock, dampening his balls when he began to move faster. Elizabeth moaning, her pussy clenching around him as he fucked her, gripping him, milking him . . .

Ah hell!

He looked down and noticed he'd been rubbing his cock through his jeans. God, next thing he'd have it in his hand, pumping it.

Before Elizabeth could return, he ducked into his own bathroom, almost ripping the zipper off his jeans to free the aching, rigid flesh, shucking the jeans in quick movements.

Yanking open the glass door of his shower, he flicked the lever, cold water blasting out, and stood underneath it, eyes closed, shivering while he willed his erection to just die, for God's sake.

THE MAIN LIVING AREA was empty when Elizabeth walked out of the guest room. The shower had done wonders and she felt ready to tackle Tom again. Subtle spices teased her nose, the mix a tantalizing blend of something Asian. Her mouth watered to thoughts of Tom's special Thai stir-fry . . . But before she could head in the direction of the kitchen to find out, she was distracted by the setting Tom had prepared for the painting.

A decadent, plush, red velvet couch, wide, with scrolled, padded arms and finely carved feet, set off by the lustrous sheen of a creamy satin backdrop threaded with gold. A six-foot butterfly palm stood sentinel over the tableau, the rich green and yellow fronds offering a striking contrast to the richness of the deep ruby red and gold-shot cream.

How the hell she'd missed it earlier . . . She'd passed Tom's studio part of the loft to get to the guest room, but the sight of a shirtless Tom had always had the ability to make certain parts of her brain short-circuit. Some things never changed.

Catching movement out of the corner of her eye, she turned to see Tom leaning against the wall watching her, arms crossed over a now-covered chest, the thin white T-shirt stretched taut, showing the toned pecs and hint of dark chest hair, jeans-clad legs lazily crossed at the ankles. God, he was gorgeous. Tall, dark and handsome just didn't do him justice. Her pulse sped up just looking at him.

His hair was damp too, the rich dark brown waves slicked back off his forehead. From the looks of it, she wasn't the only one who'd taken a quick shower. An image of him naked, water sluicing down that hard, muscled body, the hair-covered chest leading down to tight abs, the dark trail of hair arrowing down to the nest of dark curls that surrounded the thickest, most delicious—

Realizing where her eyes had landed, she blinked and looked away, embarrassed at the direction of her eyes and her thoughts, and nodded at the setting. "That's beautiful, Tom. What an amazing couch. Plenty of room for two." Her eyes widened. "I mean, Richard and me. He and I . . . Posing. Later." She rolled her eyes. "You know what I mean. It's nice, anyway. Wonderful ambience." She tugged on the end of the knotted tie of her robe. "I hope this is what you wanted—the robe. I thought you'd rather get started straightaway since we don't have much time."

His expression hardened, his jawline tense. "Actually, I thought you might like to eat first. It's nearly dinnertime. Aren't you hungry?"

"I guess. Normally I don't eat until about nine, when I remember. Just before the rush hits at the club. Some nights I don't . . ." She looked down at her robe, suddenly feeling a little too casual. "Give me a sec and I'll go get changed."

"No need." He turned and walked away. "Come on through. It's ready. We can eat in front of the fire."

Grasping the lapels of her robe together, she swallowed down her misgivings and followed him through the gothic wooden hallway doors to the open-plan living room. Nothing had changed, she realized as she looked around. The large antique stone fireplace was blazing merrily, surrounded by the same comfortable leather lounge suite offset by the richly colored Persian rug.

"Here. Take this and go get comfy."

She turned at the hand on her elbow and took the glass of red wine he offered her. She closed her eyes and sniffed, a smile spreading across her face as the fruity bouquet teased her senses.

Nestling into a corner of the large lounge, she took a sip of her wine before placing it on the coffee table, looking up in time to see Tom standing to the side of her with two large noodle bowls in his hands, fragrant steam wafting up to make her tummy rumble in anticipation.

"Hmmm," she said, inhaling as she took the bowl. "Your cooking skills haven't diminished, I see."

"Limited cooking skills." His mouth kicked up at the corner in a self-conscious grin. "My repertoire is still limited to one dish."

"Yes, but it's a very, very good dish," she encouraged, inhaling briefly before she began to twist the noodles around her fork, her mouth watering in anticipation.

He sat on the floor in front of the fire, leaning up against the lounge beside her with his legs stretched out in front of him, bare feet pointing toward the fire.

It didn't matter that he'd put on a T-shirt. Even his broad, long feet were sexy as hell. She looked down at her bowl instead, trying to concentrate on the food.

As she ate, and they talked, she tried to remember the last time she'd spent a night like this—just relaxing in front of a fire, glass of wine, wonderful food . . . She couldn't remember a single one. Not since she'd bought the club. And until now, she hadn't stopped long enough to remember what she'd been missing.

Debbie was right—she needed to get back to a more normal life. The emptiness of her current one was glaringly obvious.

"Let me take that."

She was pulled out of her thoughts, not even aware she'd wandered off mentally until she realized Tom was standing in front of her reaching for her bowl.

"Thanks. It was delicious."

"My pleasure," he said, and walked to the kitchen. She picked up her glass and finished off the last mouthful of wine, then lay back and sighed. Food. Wine. A flickering fire. It was heaven. She closed her eyes and enjoyed the feeling of total relaxation.

The couch dipped a little as Tom sat beside her on the edge of the sofa and she hummed when his fingers pushed the hair back off her forehead and then began to slowly stroke. She exhaled with the pleasure the sensation brought. Nobody had cared for her like this for a long time, not since . . . She mentally shook off the thought. Tonight she just wanted to enjoy. "I always loved it when you did that."

"I know."

She wanted to open her eyes, but she was just too comfortable, the sensation too relaxing. "Hmmm, that feels so good."

"You look beautiful lying there like that, Elizabeth. Would you mind if I sketch you?"

"Does it involve me moving? Do you need me naked?"

He chuckled, the sound warm and rich. "Talk about loaded questions. Would I be munching on my testicles for a week if I answered yes and yes?"

She laughed softly, opening one eyelid to peer up at him before turning on the sofa and pushing the cushion under her head. "Bad man. Tonight you're safe—only because you wined and dined me. Am I all right like this?" she asked, yawning.

"Stay just as you are, sweetheart. You're perfect."

A pair of warm lips pressed a kiss to her forehead, and she smiled, her eyes still closed. "Good, I don't think I could move right now if you paid me to."

The seat dipped again as he stood, and she listened as his footsteps padded away.

IT WASN'T EASY, FINDING his "zone" with an almost naked Elizabeth stretched out in front of him and a painfully hard erection to contend with, but eventually he did. He'd been sketching for an hour before it penetrated that Elizabeth had fallen asleep. The soft snores brought an affectionate smile to his face. She must have been tired. But then with the crazy hours she worked, it wasn't surprising.

The only problem was, he now needed the robe off, but didn't want to wake her. And he didn't want to wait. Knowing Elizabeth, she could sleep for hours.

Bending over her, he loosened the tie, although the knot gave him some trouble at first. As it released, he breathed a sigh of relief. Slowly, so as not to disturb her, he eased the two halves of the gown apart.

His heart started to pound, his fingers tightening on the silky fabric as her body was revealed. Christ, she was beautiful. How the hell had he let her get away from him?

Because he was a stupid fuckwit.

Turning on his heel, he continued remonstrating with himself while he picked up his pad again and tried to get comfortable in his favorite chair.

With quick, deft strokes, he began to draw. But following the gentle curve of her neck, the way her jaw led to a slightly pointy chin—her "stubborn" chin she used to call it—reminded him of the days and nights he'd spent drawing her before. The pert nose, the soft curve of her mouth, even when she was asleep.

All so achingly familiar.

When his gaze tracked lower, over the feminine little bump of her collarbone, before the first gentle swell of her breasts, he had to grit his teeth to stop his hand from shaking.

Her large nipples were flat, the dark pink circles begging for his tongue to tease them to hardness. His jaw clenched.

A series of sure strokes filled in the shape.

He quickly shifted his eyes to the noticeable ridges of her rib cage, a slight frown forming a crease between his brows. She'd lost weight. Elizabeth had always been curvy, nicely covered so that bones didn't stick out. As an artist, it was one of the things he'd found so attractive about her.

But then his personal preference was for curves. Lush, shapely, like Elizabeth. He loved running his hands over her body and feeling the flesh give underneath, molding around him, cushioning his hardness, softening as she relaxed against him.

Tracing the flare of her hips, he noticed her tummy was still more rounded than flat. He loved the soft swell. To him it was one of the feminine things about her—a hard, flat abdomen on a woman was about as sexy as an ingrown toenail. How many nights after they'd made love had he curled around her, legs entwined, as he caressed and stroked it? Maybe he was weird, but to his mind, if he wanted to fuck a hard muscled body with a six-pack of abs, he might as well fuck a guy. For just a moment, the thought came to mind of her tummy swelling in another way—fuller, the skin stretched over the tiny babe she carried. Thoughts of taking her, making love to her as he ran his hands over the proof of their love . . . their child. The surge of possessiveness, of almost primal protectiveness that powered through him took him by surprise. He blinked his eyes and the image shattered.

Gripping the pencil a little harder, he tracked lower, aware for the first time that the crinkly black hairs previously gracing her plump mound were almost gone. In their place a thin strip that led between her closed legs. Led to paradise.

Christ! The pencil snapped in his hand. When had that happened? And for whom? Jealousy surged through him. He should have questioned Richard more closely about her "love life" when he had the chance. But then it was ridiculous for him to think that a woman like Elizabeth wouldn't be pursued by men. She'd probably been beating them off with a stick, while he'd been sitting around sulking like an adolescent with a chip on his shoulder.

She moved, tilting her upper body a little so that she lay partly on her back. He groaned softly as the puffed lips of her mostly bare pussy became more visible. His mouth watered to taste her, to run his tongue up the pink slit and lick until she came.

He dropped lower in his seat. Damn, his cock was so hard the constriction of his jeans was killing him. Two years of celibacy were now having disastrous effects on his body. He definitely had another appointment with his shower gel. Just as soon as he finished . . .

Dropping the now useless remnants of his pencil, he picked up another, sketching quickly to finish the drawing. He really needed to cover her up again.

Then another cold shower.

Placing his pad on the floor, he stood to lean over her, intending to pull the robe closed, when she moved. And stretched.

He froze, his hands suspended over her. Breath stopped as he waited for her to open her eyes.

Part of him wanted her to. Wanted her to watch as he leaned down to tongue her nipples into hard peaks.

But she didn't. Instead he looked down at her arms now lying back over her head, her breasts pulled up, the firm curves tempting him so much that he had to swallow before he drooled all over her.

Kneeling on the floor beside her, he lowered his head, his

eyes fastened on the tempting flesh of the dusky areola. His tongue flicked out, tracing a damp line around the edge, the circles growing smaller and smaller until he rimmed the tip. He paused, exhaling warm breaths over the dampened flesh, inhaling the sweet scent of Elizabeth—a muted hint of jasmine, so definably her that his cock pounded in response.

Eyes fastened on her sweet face, he opened his lips over the beaded tip of her nipple, sucking gently. He bit back a groan when the nub hardened, lengthening under his lips. She moaned in her sleep, her body moving, her back arching slightly as if searching for more.

"Tom . . ." Her whispered plea nearly made his heart stop. He searched her face, still rubbing the hard nipple over his tongue, expecting her to open her eyes. At this point he didn't care. He wanted her so much. Could she possibly be dreaming about him? Not some other guy, but him?

"More, Tom. More . . ." Her voice petered away on a soft little moan as he surrendered and flicked the tip with his tongue then took a little more, tugging a little harder as she began to writhe beneath him. Switching sides, he tended to the other nipple, lapping at the sweetness of her skin, drinking in the music of her breathy sighs and pleas. Her nipples had always been her most sensitive spot—she could orgasm from him sucking on them alone—and he loved them.

When he heard her breathing accelerate, quick little puffs of air passing her lips, he pulled back, looking down at her, feeling the hunger for her that had never been far away, gnawing at him. All it took was a thought of her . . . The robe was now fully parted, showing every inch of silky skin.

A glance at the bared flesh of her labia showed the faint glisten of her juices on the dark pink lips. The musky scent of her arousal wafted up to him, pulling him closer until his mouth was over her delicious pussy and his tongue was swiping a slow line through the silky skin of her folds.

Fuck! He closed his eyes, the taste of her spilling over his tongue. Her legs parted as he looked at her delicious cunt, and he breathed deeply. God, this was heaven.

Moving to the end of the couch, he positioned himself between her legs, taking care not to disturb her.

Letting his arms bear the weight, he positioned himself above her, leaning down to lick her again, running his tongue over the velvety smoothness of her smooth labia. So soft, so sweet. Nectar. Ambrosia.

Plump, swollen, the flushed lips made him ache to work his cock inside her. But not now. From the sounds leaving her mouth, the excited shivers over her skin, she needed this. And he couldn't deny her. Would never deny her again.

His tongue slid inside the sweet slit, and he couldn't stop the hum that rumbled out of his chest. Keeping his eyes on Elizabeth's face, he licked, sucked, lapped and nibbled until her hips arched off the sofa, closer to his mouth, nudging against his lips, telling him of her need for more.

He lifted his face, slowly easing a single finger between the slick folds, moving it back and forward, gritting his teeth at the way her muscles gripped him. But he knew when he'd found her sweet spot. Her body began to move, just small undulations, in time with the rubbing of his finger, continuous little pants leaving her lips.

She was close. It struck him just how well he knew her body—the signs, the sounds, the way she started to clench and release on him when she was about to come. As he inserted another finger, the lips of her pussy parted, revealing the swollen nub of her clit.

His face positioned over her again, he flicked and licked the sensitive little button, feeling her body begin to shudder under his mouth and fingers, the wetness building, making his fingers slick with her juices.

Wrapping his lips around her clit, he sucked, not hard, but enough to push her over the edge, and her body stiffened before twitching in time with her contractions as he continued to thrust gently. Gradually the spasming around his fingers eased and she lay still, her breathing slowly returning to normal.

His body ached with the need to move over her and slide his aching cock inside her sweet hole, feel her sheath swallow him up until he was buried up to her womb.

But if he didn't move away now, he'd be inside her and pounding away before he could stop himself.

With trembling hands, he pulled the edges of her robe together, gritting his teeth as a hand brushed against her breast, his palm curving around the silky mound for one brief, exquisite moment before tying the belt loosely, his hands fumbling over the knot. Her body shifted, the movement slight, almost imperceptible, and he stroked her forehead, smoothing over the skin with butterfly-light touches, knowing how it calmed her.

"Shhh, sleep, Elizabeth," he whispered at her ear, his tone soothing, gentle.

Grabbing the afghan off the back of the lounge, he draped it over her, tucking it in at the sides before leaning down to place a kiss on her forehead.

"Love you, sweetheart."

He straightened and stepped back. After one final lingering glance, he turned and left the room.

As HIS BEDROOM DOOR clicked closed behind him, Elizabeth's eyes blinked open and she drew in a deep shuddering breath, exhaling a single word, filled with pain and longing. "Tom . . ." Her arms lowered, her fingers clutching the blanket, as a single tear, followed by another and then another, tracked down the side of her cheek, slipping off her face to dampen the lock of hair beneath.

With the back of her hand, she brushed the trail of wetness from her cheeks. Her mind was confused, her jumbled emotions taking much longer to settle than her body. She knew better than anyone what a tender, giving lover Tom could be, but what had just occurred . . . There had been no artifice, no power, no advantage to be gained from it. Behind the gentle caring, she had sensed his need for her, and even without his final whispered words, the love communicated in the gentleness of his caresses.

It was that same need for him, for his touch, that had made her continue to feign sleep. With the first stroke of his fingers, she had awoken from the light sleep she'd drifted into. But with her eyes closed, she could pretend nothing had changed, and the dreamlike moment wouldn't be shattered.

She loved him—still. It was something she had never denied—not to herself, anyway. But could things be different between them? Could their two worlds ever meet, or would the same conflicts drive them apart again? And would she be able to survive the heartbreak again if it did?

THE WARM SUNLIGHT ON her face roused Elizabeth and she sat up, rubbing her eyes as she tossed off the afghan blanket Tom had covered her with the night before. As she swung her legs off the lounge, her sleepy gaze landed on the folded note on the coffee table. She fingered the note, thinking about the previous night. Wondering what the day would hold. With a shake of her head, she pushed the thought away. Time would tell. She opened the note to discover Tom had gone for a jog, and for her to help herself to whatever she wanted.

Well, what she wanted was a nice, long, hot shower. Feeling the chill in the air, she dressed comfortably in a pair of sweatpants and a thick, wooly jumper, pulling on a thick pair of socks to keep her feet warm on the polished wood floors.

Hunger wasn't an issue, since she rarely ate breakfast at the club, so instead she grabbed a cup of black coffee from the coffeepot keeping warm on the kitchen counter. The rich scent of Tom's personal blend teased her senses, and that first sip made her hum with delight. There was nothing in the world quite like a good cup of coffee.

Not knowing how long Tom would be gone, since she had no idea when he'd actually left, she wandered around the loft, noticing how little had changed since she'd been away. She was on her way up to the garden seat on the roof when she paused before the staircase, noticing the open door to the smaller room that had originally been intended as a spare bedroom, but had long been Tom's storeroom for his completed or semi-completed paintings.

Curiosity ate at her. Refusing to consider it snooping, an innate inquisitiveness to see what he had worked on during her absence had her feet moving into the dark, shuttered room. A quick tug on the cord, and the wooden slat blinds opened to flood the room with daylight.

Knowing Tom's preference for grouping his paintings in chronological order, she started with the rack furthest from the door, recognizing, as she flicked through the first few, paintings he had completed prior to their original introduction.

The next two racks held those he had undertaken while she lived with him. It was like plunging into the past, to a happier time, his choice of colors rich, vibrant—happy colors. Particular favorites of hers were the ones with children—he loved to capture their *joie de vivre*, that playful curiosity or impish mischievousness. In complete contrast were the ones he'd done of her—richly colored, highly sensual, whether whimsical poses or those charged with erotic nuance. Even though she recalled posing for every single one, it was, as always, disconcerting seeing herself through his eyes. The woman in the paintings was so different from the one she faced in the mirror—more earthy, seductive—he even made her look beautiful.

However, it was the final two racks that held the most interest for her. She paused a moment with her hand on the first painting, almost reticent, now that she was here, to pull it back and see what it held. What had inspired him? Or more importantly, who? That thought had trepidation skittering through her, her heart rate pounding, her breathing picking up as an uncomfortable rush of adrenaline flooded her system. Who had replaced her? Which woman had been responsible for firing his passion for his art? Elizabeth felt a stab of unreasonable jealousy at whoever had taken her place—she had left Tom, after all, not the other way around.

But from her own experience with Tom, she knew better than anyone how he unleashed the passion he poured into his erotic paintings. She couldn't count the days or nights he had made love to her, bringing her to orgasm, over and over, only to carry her sated body through to his studio, placing her on his soft old couch to slumber or watch as he attacked his canvas with single-minded focus, waking her hours later as he carried her into bed and wrapped himself around her before total exhaustion took him and he slept soundly.

Did she really want to see? Whatever or whoever had been his "inspiration" once she left? She knew it would be like gazing into a part of his soul—a part she hadn't been a part of.

Her hand tightened on the wooden mount. Taking a deep breath, she made her decision.

Pulling it toward her, she looked down at a painting of a woman. The background was muted in shades of gray, the mood one of sadness, despair. Rather than a full figure, it was a portrait, the woman partially turned away, looking back over her shoulder. But it was the expression on her face—the pain, the hurt almost tangible so that she reached without thinking to touch her, wanting to soothe the pain she knew she was feeling. She knew that pain, that despair. It mirrored her own the day she had walked away from Tom.

It was, in fact, her.

The thought that he had painted her rocked her. But to have captured so accurately what she'd been feeling . . . So much of that day was now a blur, details muffled by the emotional devastation of leaving him. But consumed by her own pain, she'd been unable to contemplate the aftermath for Tom. Now she knew. He'd dealt with it the only way he knew how.

With a distracted movement, she brushed at the tear that had wound its way down her cheek, breathing deeply to stem the imminent flood of more.

Steeling herself, she flicked through the others, painting after painting. A dozen or more.

Her. With one or two exceptions, they were all of her.

As with the first one, he had chosen key moments in their lives together. And she recognized every single one—the happy ones, the quiet ones, those moments where they were so deeply in love that nothing and no one else mattered.

They had each dealt with the separation in different ways. And while she had never been able to let go of her feelings for him, quite possibly it had been the same for Tom. Maybe he did still love her after all.

So where did that leave them now?

She turned and left the room, snapping the blind shut and plunging the room once more into darkness. As she walked up the staircase and stood up on the roof, looking over the sooty London skyline, feeling the wind buffet her, the brisk chill of the breeze clearing the emotional miasma of the past from her head and thrusting her back into the present, she pondered what to do.

She could wait for Tom to make a move. If he loved her as he'd said, and wanted her back, then he had to be prepared to face what had forced them apart. It would require him putting her first, even before his art, to resolve the issues with his family. Could he do it? Was it, as before, asking more of him than he could give?

Or . . . A thought occurred to her and a small smile tipped her lips as she raised the mug and took a long sip of coffee. Perhaps Tom's motivation for action lay with another member of his family.

Richard. In a few days he'd be back. And knowing Richard as she did, it was highly unlikely he'd behave once they were both naked—especially with Tom watching. The only other time she and Richard had posed together had nearly driven Tom over the edge watching Richard's hands wandering all over her body, ostensibly trying to "get comfortable." Until "getting comfortable" had involved a hand cupping one of her breasts. That would have been more than enough for Tom, until Richard had begun to "innocently" fondle her nipple. In less than an hour, the sitting had been over, Richard was bundled into the lift, and Tom had been fucking her with a frenzy on the rug in the living room, where he'd tackled her as she ran away from him after teasing him about the erection he'd developed watching them.

Maybe she wouldn't have to do a thing . . .

FOUR

GOOD LORD! THOUGHT RICHARD. The two of them were worse than a couple of teenagers. Sneaking longing glances at each other when they thought the other one wasn't looking. And the sexual tension . . . Hell, it had been so thick since he arrived, it was nearly choking him. Whatever had happened before he got there, it sure as hell wasn't what he'd hoped would happen once they had a bit of time alone together. Elizabeth wasn't saying, even when he managed to get her alone, for the short spells when Tom finally left her for ten minutes while he showered. And Tom . . . He was strung tighter than a drum.

Still, something had happened. Something they obviously hadn't talked about, judging from the little pantomime being played out in front of him. Although, from the way Tom hovered over her constantly, finding any excuse to touch her, however innocently, he was at least moving in the right direction.

But time was running out for them. In a few days, as per her contract, Elizabeth would be back at her club and Tom would be alone once more, head stuck in a canvas while the love of his life walked out that door—for the second time.

For a guy who wasn't backward in coming forward about taking what he wanted from life, Tom had royally screwed up with Elizabeth from the word "go."

But not this time. On that point Richard was determined. Not if he had anything to say—or do—about it.

He flicked a glance between the two of them. Tom's butt was perched on his stool, long legs stretched out in front, as he fiddled with his pencils again on the round table beside him. Tension, anger, stress, whatever—he always fiddled with those damned pencils. Sharpening them, lining them up, sorting them . . .

Normally it drove him nuts, but this time he at least knew the reason.

Elizabeth was another matter. He couldn't quite work out what was going on in that mischievous mind of hers. She was nervous about something—he just couldn't figure out what. And as if the drink of water she'd just grabbed from the kitchen was going to help quiet those jumpy little nerves he could see written all over her face. Richard smiled to himself.

It was time for Elizabeth to get naked.

For Elizabeth *and him* to get naked.

Together.

Where good old Tom could watch. Jealous as hell that it wasn't him on the lounge with Elizabeth.

And Richard intended for him to get an eyeful.

He planned to ratchet up that jealousy until it jerked Tom out of that damn stasis he was in regarding Elizabeth and into some positive action.

Reclining back on the armrest, fingers linked behind his head, he looked at the two of them and rolled his eyes. It was pretty damn obvious, to him at least, that they both wanted nothing more than to fuck like bunnies until they blew each other's brains out. However neither one seemed prepared to make the first move.

So, that left him—good old Richard. If he didn't love them both so much, he'd walk out now and leave them to it. But no, if two people were meant to be together, it was these two. And he would do his darnedest to help. Besides, he was really going to enjoy this.

Standing up, he flicked the studs on his jeans, turning away as he bent over and shucked them down his legs, off his feet, tossing them onto the floor out of the way.

As he straightened he caught a glimpse of Elizabeth's wide eyes at his choice of underwear, quietly amused by the nervous little glances she threw from his butt to Tom.

And Tom. Hell, he could give that moody geezer from *Pride and Prejudice* lessons in brooding. Well, not for much longer . . .

Slowly, dragging it out for maximum effect, he slid his underpants down his legs, watching Elizabeth closely as he gave a little wiggle for effect. A smirk tipped his lips when she rolled her eyes at him. Gee, and that was the thanks he got for putting on his silky black G-string just for her. With a flick and a grin, he kicked it to land on his jeans.

"Ready, sweet pea?" Richard said to Elizabeth and winked, earning him a muttered, exasperated "Rich-*ard!*" Grasping her shoulders, he steered her backward until she reached the velvet lounge, pushing her down until her bottom touched the seat.

"Now you just lie back and let me do all the work, okay?" He sat down beside her.

"Richard, I don't think—"

"Good," he said, cutting her off as he eased her head back onto the tasseled pillow. "That's your biggest problem right there—thinking."

He caught her widened eyes looking down between their bodies at his growing erection. Even he was surprised—and delighted—by the display. Talk about running up the flagpole. "Now, don't worry about ol' Willy there. He's got a mind of his own, and besides, no man with a pulse could be in the position I'm in and not get a hard-on, love. Anyway, I'm sure Tom will draw me to be a pencil-dick or something in retaliation for putting my hands on you."

Richard grinned as she chuckled, and brushed the vagrant strands of hair back from her face. "It's only good old Richard. So just relax and trust me, okay?" She nodded. "That's the way."

He turned to Tom, seeing the warning darkness in his eyes, the rigid set of his jaw, his fingers gripping the pencil until the knuckles whitened. From the looks of that thunderous expression, a few molars were going to be sacrificed before Richard was done. Tom really needed to let go of some of that pressure. Learn how to vent. All that "stiff upper lip" crap would just give him an ulcer.

"We'll try a few poses, Tom. You just sketch away and let us know when we hit one that does it for you. Okay?" Richard knew damn well none of this was "okay" with Tom, since it involved any man but Tom being naked with his woman, but that was his tough luck.

Without waiting for an answer, Richard turned back to Elizabeth. *Poses. Right.* He doubted Tom would be drawing too much very shortly anyway . . . "Now, Elizabeth my lovely, what say you and I get nice and cozy?"

Positioning Elizabeth so that she was comfortable—arms draped loosely over her head, legs extended but slightly spread, one knee bent—Richard waited until she had settled against the tasseled cushions, lying back in sybaritic splendor. God, what a delicious sight!

Then, locking her gaze with his, he reached for the tie of her silky robe, slowly working the knot free. For a brief moment, she tensed, her eyes startled.

"Come now, love," Richard whispered, seeking to settle her, "this isn't the first time we've done this. Though I daresay after today's little effort it will be the last." He winked at her, her eyes going wide until she got his meaning. Or *thought* she got his meaning. If she had any idea what he had planned, she'd likely knee him in the balls. Regardless, he felt his cock harden further with the sensual, slumberous look that came over her eyes.

He had modeled with Elizabeth once before for Tom. Two years ago. A couple of hours of having her luscious bod reclining back against his chest, bare as the day she was born. Even though it had been Tom's suggestion, he had been so pissed off at seeing her wrapped up in Richard's arms, he'd finished the sketches in just over an hour.

But Richard had always had a soft spot for her. She had a fresh, open way of looking at life that just made a person feel good about themselves. In fact, the only thing that had kept him from stepping in when his fool cousin let Elizabeth go was the knowledge that some day it would come to this. Or he would have snapped her up the second she walked out on Tom.

"Don't move." Keeping his touch gentle, his movements slow, he reached for the robe. The fabric could easily have slipped open on its own, but instead he parted it, ensuring the slippery fabric teased her nipples on the way before he released it.

He was rewarded by a soft indrawn breath. Moving to his hands and knees, he leaned over her, watching her eyes almost cross as he drew closer.

He placed a soft kiss on her lips, noting how warm, how soft they felt under his before he nibbled along her jawline to her ear. Down lower, his cock hardened further and he could only imagine the view Tom must be getting.

"Watch Tom, love, and don't take your eyes off him," he whispered in her ear. He pulled back a little, noticing she watched him still. "You know I love you, sweet pea, and I won't hurt you. But trust me and keep your eyes on Tom. No matter what I do," he whispered for her ears only.

Her eyes swung back to Tom. He couldn't see him, but he could guess what he looked like, judging from the slight elevation of Elizabeth's breathing.

Lapping his tongue along the velvety skin of her neck, down over the gentle swell of a full breast, he licked up the underside, closing his eyes briefly at the sweet smell of her skin. A soft, ultrafeminine scent . . . Whatever it was, it was Elizabeth all over—warm, sexy, delicious.

Giving himself over to the enjoyment that awaited him for as long as he had, he ran the fingers of a hand up her side, noting how soft, how sensually rich her skin felt, before finally cupping the relaxed swell of a breast, massaging it in his palm. Closing his lips over the other nub, now tight and puckered, he sucked, light tugs, closing his eyes and moaning softly as he enjoyed the taste, the texture as it rolled over his tongue.

WHAT HAD HAPPENED?

As instructed, Elizabeth watched Tom. Trying unsuccessfully to block the sensations that shot through her body like lightning with every tug, every nip of the sensitive tip under Richard's lips.

But Tom . . . The second Richard moved over her, a change had come over him. Jaw clenched. Body tense. Eyes, the blue so dark as to be almost black, swirling with hunger. A wild, possessive hunger.

But more than that, need. The same tale of insatiable need she imagined her own told.

Richard shifted. Moving. Rimming the other nipple before nipping it sharply. And on her indrawn gasp, the jerk of her body, Tom jerked too. Her eyes floated lower, unable to miss the strain caused by the swelling in his jeans.

Good, he was turned on. Annoyed as hell. Furious, judging from his expression. But turned on to see what Richard was doing. To her.

Her breath caught as Richard sucked harder and she began to pant, trying to draw more oxygen into her lungs.

Tom's sketchpad dropped to the floor, her body jumping in response to the sharpness of the noise as it hit the parquetry floor.

Richard shifted again. Lower, his wicked tongue flicking a

damp trail down her ribs, tracing each line until she arched against his mouth, trails of goose bumps following in the wake of his lips.

God, how much more could she take—could Tom take? His breathing was deeper, harsher, his eyes blazing fire at her. And still, no words came from his lips.

When Richard left the dip of her belly button, the rasp of his chin leading the way over delicate flesh, gentle hands parting her thighs further, she tensed, knowing what would come.

And that first breath, that initial brush of his tongue, so hot, down the damp folds of her sex, had her arching up, a shuddering groan releasing as she let free the breath she'd been holding.

The pencil in Tom's fingers snapped, a piece of it flying across the room.

And as Richard's tongue took a long, slow swipe, her eyelids fluttered shut, unable to stand the torment, the undeniable, torturous pleasure of feeling one man pleasure her while the man she loved watched.

It was an escape, shutting them out to submit to the sensations.

Her surrender.

"Eyes open, Elizabeth! Dammit!"

Startled out of her sensuous torpor, she blinked. Tom now stood, staring at them intently, ferociously. Lust and desire etched into every line of his body. He had always been the sexually dominant one in their relationship. It was one of the things that made her so hot. And now it looked like her hungry tiger was back.

"Watch me, baby." Tom's eyes darkened, his nostrils flaring as he stepped closer and caught her scent. Her clit tingled, sending the juices flowing at the commanding tone of his voice, confirmed by the moan as Richard lapped faster, pushed deeper at her sex. "He told you that, didn't he? Knew how fucking crazy it would make me, seeing another man touch you, lick you, kiss that sweet cunt that's mine. So you watch me, Elizabeth, and see what it's fucking doing to me."

In spite of the darting thrusts of Richard's tongue inside her, she watched, her eyes wide, as Tom slid open the zipper on his jeans, and his cock, hard, thick, already weeping from the small slit, fell out into his palm.

A small, hungry whimper left her lips as he began to stroke. From root to tip, the movement slow, the grip firm. As he watched her.

CHRIST! TOM HAD NEVER seen anything as beautiful as Elizabeth. Right then. Her face flushed, the rosy color traveling down her neck, over the delicious mounds of her breasts. The rich brown strands of hair flowing around her head like ripples of silk. He could spend a lifetime trying and never capture the many facets that made up Elizabeth's beauty.

Full breasts wobbling as her chest rose and fell as she panted, short, sharp little breaths puffing through the teeth biting into her bottom lip as her excitement escalated.

A few times when they were younger, he and Richard had shared a woman. But that was different. He hadn't been in love with any of them. And though one side of him wanted to kill Richard for doing this, for touching her like he was, some twisted part of him wanted to see Elizabeth's pleasure as another man took her. But with her eyes only on him.

That was the key. That acknowledgment that her pleasure came from and through him. He needed that. And more. He needed all of her. Needed everything she had to give.

Stripping quickly, he felt satisfaction flare inside him as her eyes grew heavy-lidded, the long lashes fluttering once or twice as her gaze landed on his cock. Licking her lips and leaving a glistening, tantalizing swipe across the reddened, swollen flesh.

Moving closer, a step, two. Until the scent of her arousal filtered up to him, torturing him, the familiar fragrance weakening him so that he had to lock his knees.

Her skin glistened now with a light sheen, continuous little panting moans coming from deep inside her chest that shredded his control.

Richard raised his head, his lips shiny from Elizabeth's pussy, his eyes dark and impatient, his eyebrow raised in an unspoken dare.

Jaw clenched, Tom nodded. Watched a moment longer as Richard slipped a finger inside the tight sheath. Then withdrew, working two fingers back inside before lowering his head again to flick at Elizabeth's clit.

Her hips lifted, pushing up against Richard's mouth and fingers.

Tom began to stroke his cock again. "You thinking of me, baby? Wishing it was me?"

"Please," she panted. "Please, Tom."

He grasped his cock hard at the base, waiting until the warning throb eased off. "Shhh, baby. We'll take care of you." He reached a hand down to caress and cup the side of her face. "You want this, sweetheart?" Still stroking the hot cock in his hands, he inclined his head at it, waiting for her answer.

Biting her lip, she nodded.

"Not good enough, sweetheart. I need to hear the words. Give me the words, baby."

Before she could speak, a ragged moan was torn from her as Richard reached deep inside her, his fingers thrusting faster. "I want . . . I want . . . Tom, please. Give it to me."

Christ, he couldn't wait any longer himself. Straddling the arm of the lounge, he cupped her face in his hands. "Open up those sweet lips, baby. That's it." He gritted his teeth against the shocking intensity of that first heated touch. "Take me. Take all of me." Sinking with slow thrusts into the delicious warmth. Her lips tightening around the aching flesh as her tongue flicked the underneath.

His knees swayed. Hell, she had the most magic mouth. Always had.

"Now, suck it. Come on, hard, sweetheart. I need it so fucking hard." As he began to fuck her, those lips stretched around the thickness of his shaft, her moans of pleasure vibrated along the length of his dick. More than sexual hunger ate at him, and words he'd sworn he'd never say to another woman after she left him, leaving his life empty, his heart devastated, escaped from his traitorous lips. "I need *you*, baby," he whispered. "Oh fuck, I need you so much."

Fiery lances of sensation shot up his legs, down his spine, the overload of stimulation centering in the tight sac between his legs. Panting, he shut his eyes, shaking his head to flick off the sweat that threatened to blind him. He opened them with a snap when he felt her hands on his butt, kneading the taut flesh, fingers trailing down the crevice teasingly to push against the tightness of his asshole.

"Enough!" he grunted.

Freeing his grip on her face, Tom grasped her hands and pulled them away, backing up so that his cock slipped free of her mouth, the bobbing, pulsing length shiny and wet.

"Richard," he gritted out. "I take it you're prepared?"

A devilish grin creased his cousin's lips. "Like a Boy Scout."

"Move. Come around behind me."

Alone on the lounge, Elizabeth half sat, her body trembling, the arms that supported her shaking noticeably. She hadn't come. Richard wouldn't have let her, but damn if she didn't look ready to explode. Tom knew his Elizabeth, intimately familiar with every signal her body put out. He reached down to stroke her cheek, his thumb wiping over her bottom lip so that it pouted at him. "This is what you want, sweetheart? Because if you do, I really want to give it to you."

She nodded. "Yes. Yes, both of you."

He bent and kissed her, hard. Thrusting his tongue inside her mouth as she arched up to him, her arms looping around his neck, holding him tight.

Lips still joined, he lay down on the lounge, pulling Elizabeth with him so that she lay over him. The wetness flowed from her pussy, the heat scorching his cock. And he had yet to get inside her. She was going to set his cock on fire.

With a final lick over her lip, he eased back from the kiss, pure satisfaction surging through him at her sexy, disheveled appearance above him.

"Hands on my shoulders, sweetheart," Tom said softly. "Brace yourself."

Her eyes were so deep, the blue so clear he could drown in them. His heart beat harder as he looked at her, seeing her eyes go glassy, one single tear welling up to topple over the lid and slide down her cheek.

"I need you too, Tom. Fuck me. Please, God, fuck me."

"Oh sweetheart, I'll give you whatever you need. Always." He moved her hips, lifting and positioning her until the head of his cock was kissing the lips of her vagina. The second she felt the tip at her opening, she rocked her hips, a grunt leaving his chest as half his length was swallowed up in the searing heat.

"Oh sweetheart, God, you feel like heaven." She was tight around him, the muscles inside flushed with blood, making the channel narrow. He gripped her hips harder to stop her from hurting herself as she tried to push down on him. "Slowly . . . that's it . . . yes, there's no rush, baby . . ." Her inner muscles tightened around him, nearly cutting off the circulation in his cock. "Ease up, sweetheart. Loosen those muscles so I can move, okay?" He sighed when she relaxed slightly, allowing him to work deeper until he was fully seated. He heard the crinkle of foil, caught Richard's eye over Elizabeth's shoulder. Sweat broke out on his brow as she rubbed her pelvis against his, seeking stimulation for her clit.

Her movements stilled, her eyes going wide as she felt Richard move in behind her and touch her.

"Just relax, love," Richard said as he nuzzled her ear, his lubricated finger easing inside the tight hole. Sliding in and out, relaxing the muscles, accustoming them to his touch, to the feel of being penetrated anally.

"Do you have any idea how beautiful you look to us, that gorgeous body just waiting for the pleasure we can give it?" He turned her head to kiss her, her lips swollen, her tongue searching for his hungrily.

A second finger joined the first, sliding easily now as she surrendered to the sensation, rocking slowly on Tom's cock, pushing back onto Richard's fingers. He broke the kiss, panting against her neck. "And it will be pleasure, love. So much pleasure . . . for all of us."

"You talk . . . too much . . . Richard," she gasped as Richard withdrew his fingers and lined up his cock at the pouting little hole. "Been telling you that for *years!*" Her voice rose on the final syllable as he nudged and pushed past the tight ring of muscles until just the head was crowned. Her ass clenched on him so that he couldn't move and Richard gritted his teeth against the exquisite shafts of pleasure that raced up his cock.

"Oh my God!" she panted.

Richard's grip tightened on her hips in direct relation to the gripping around his cock. "Fuck, Tom, she's choking me." And she was, but along with the tightness was the most indescribable warmth and tantalizing friction that shot straight to his balls.

"Come here, sweetheart." Tom eased Elizabeth closer to him, holding her face while he bussed his lips over hers. Whatever Tom was doing worked, because Richard felt the relaxation spread through her body, the clenching grip on his cock easing so he could slide more freely. A sigh of relief left his lips.

Three more slow and easy thrusts and he was buried inside her, his groin rubbing against the warm cheeks of her ass. He leaned back and skimmed his hands over the rounded globes.

"Tom . . . hell, Elizabeth has the most fucking beautiful ass." He glanced over Elizabeth's shoulder, catching Tom's eye, seeing the strain his cousin was feeling to not move before she was ready for them.

A nod passed between them. In tandem they began to move, timing their thrusts so that as one pulled out, the other plunged in. Over and over, the sounds of their bodies joining, the hungry sucking noises as Elizabeth's cunt swallowed Tom's cock each time, feeling the vibration and rub of Tom's cock against the ultrathin wall separating them.

And Elizabeth . . . Her moans, her broken, stuttered pleas as she lay between them, unable to move, only able to feel, to enjoy, her cries to them, begging, pleading to let her come.

Hell, he hoped it happened soon. He wasn't sure how much longer he could last.

Reaching up, running his hands up over the soft skin of her back and around to her breasts, Richard palmed them briefly, before rolling the nipples in his fingers, pinching them hard, feeling the jerk shoot through her body in response to the small bite of pain.

He tensed, gritting his teeth, his body rigid as she tried to take control and pushed back against him on the down stroke, an impatient "More!" forced from her lips as she gasped underneath him, her body shaking as the first tremors of her orgasm began to tear through her, building, her body jerking between them.

And then she was there, a keening wail of pleasure piercing the air as her channel and her ass muscles clamped around them. The pinching, clenching of her ass ripped Richard's control away. Going deep once more and tensing, holding it, he reared back, holding himself flush against her buttocks, his fingers tightening on her hips as his cock exploded inside her, pumping and pulsing in an endless stream until he was drained, shaking from the power of his release. The tip of Tom's cock rubbed against his through the thin barrier as he, too, thrust deep and tensed, roaring as he blasted deep inside her cunt.

Exhausted, Elizabeth had already collapsed onto Tom's chest, draped over him, gasping for breath. *Christ al-bloody-mighty!* Richard knew how she felt. Panting, he held himself above her, his rigid arms shaking as they kept him suspended until he felt able to withdraw, holding the condom tight to the base of his cock as his rapidly softening erection slipped free.

A shaky step back from the lounge, and Richard looked down at the two of them. Elizabeth was still collapsed over Tom's chest. Tom's arms now wrapped tight around her, holding her close as he murmured to her.

A look passed between Richard and his cousin as they both glanced at the woman they had shared, but, Richard knew, never would again.

With a wry smile, he picked up his clothes and stumbled into Tom's bathroom for a shower.

When he returned fifteen minutes later, hair still dripping, he noticed that Elizabeth had moved, now lying beside Tom on the lounge, eyes closed, her breathing returned to normal as she snuggled in close. Tom stroking her hair as his chin rested on her head.

With a parting glance at the two of them, he opened the door to the lift and left, a tired but satisfied smile creasing his face.

FIVE

ELIZABETH CAME AWAKE TO the feel of cool sheets beneath her and a warm body surrounding her like a blanket. They were in Tom's room, on his huge king-sized futon. Richard was gone. Through the skylight, she could see that night had fallen.

Behind her, an erection prodded at her backside.

"Feel like a bath?"

"Hmmm," she murmured, her body feeling deliciously satiated, "but I'd have to move."

"I could carry you . . ."

"Or . . ." She lifted her leg over his so that his cock slipped along the crease of her buttocks, nudging at the lips of her pussy. She shifted slightly to get a better position. "We could just stay here, and you could—"

She bit down on a moan as she felt him fill her from behind. "Definitely just stay here," she gasped as he began to rock inside her.

One hand began to caress her nipple, the other one moving between her legs to rub soft circles around her clit, the arc of tingling fire shooting along every nerve ending between her nipple and the ultrasensitive bud at the top of her slit.

His lips nuzzled at her neck, nipping a path to her ear.

"I love you. I've never stopped loving you, sweetheart," he moaned against the shell of her ear.

As the slow orgasm built between them, she leaned back against him, resting her head in the crook of his shoulder and closed her eyes as a single tear leaked between her lashes and skidded down her cheek. "And I love you, Tom," she whispered, her breath catching as the gentle tremors peaked and passed between them, his arms tightening around her as they rode out the gentle release.

A few minutes later he still hadn't eased his hold on her—she could feel the tension in his body, and turned in his arms. The look on his face was serious—his "thinking" face.

She ran her fingers over his brow, smoothing the lines away. "Hey, what's up?"

He grasped her fingers and kissed the tips, then held her hand against his chest so that she could feel the beat of his heart.

"I'm just wondering if you can ever forgive me . . . enough to give me—us—another chance."

Could she? In spite of what had gone before, she could tell this was a different Tom. He'd changed, matured. For that matter, she admitted, they both had. And while putting her heart on the line again was a risk, was the alternative—life without him—any better? It had been a bleak, lonely couple of years. There had been no other men—how could there be when she'd never stopped loving him? And now, lying in the shelter of his arms, knowing he still loved her, going back to being alone seemed even darker than before. For the first time in two years she felt warm again, happy. Content in a way that went soul deep. "It won't be easy, Tom. We need to talk about things this time—as equals. But we could try."

He buried his head in her shoulder, a long shuddering breath warming her neck. "God, I've missed you, sweetheart. So much. Trust me, it will be different this time. I promise you that."

As he hugged her tight against him, she felt hope. For the first time in two years, the future seemed brighter.

SINGING IN TIME WITH the music blaring from the radio, Elizabeth turned the gas flame off, and lifted the last two slices of French toast out of the pan, sliding them onto a plate to keep warm in the oven.

God, she felt great. As though she were surrounded by a big bubble of happiness. And if Tom didn't hurry up and get out of the shower, she'd say to hell with the French toast and go join him.

As she closed the oven door, the intercom phone rang on the wall beside the refrigerator, and Elizabeth stepped over to answer it, knowing it could only be one person. "Sara?"

"Yes, lass. It's me."

"What's wrong?"

"Just a warning," Sara said in a rush. "You have compan—"

The rest of Sara's words were drowned out.

"What is the meaning of this? And who the dickens are you?"

Surprised at the snappish female voice behind her, Elizabeth spun around. A tall, elegant woman, dressed in clothes that Elizabeth estimated at a glance represented at least a month's wages to most people, stood glowering at her, her eyes widening briefly before narrowing as recognition followed. "You! What are *you* doing here?"

Wonderful. Tom's mother Caroline. Just what she needed. Elizabeth quickly said her thanks to Sara and hung up the phone.

"Hello, Lady Danville. It's been such a long time." *Not quite long enough though . . .*

"Elizabeth." The way Caroline said her name, that affected upper-class drawl with a barely hidden sneer, always managed to make her feel like a peasant. Obviously Caroline's disposition toward her and the "risk" she potentially posed to her darling son hooking up with one of the bevy of debutantes she kept pushing his way, hadn't improved any. Even if Caroline had only believed she was Tom's model, her opinion that her darling son could do better was one she'd had little compunction in voicing, even in front of Elizabeth.

But she was not going to let it get her down. Not today.

"Take a seat. I'll let Tom know you're here."

She escaped to Tom's bedroom, glad to see him coming out of the bathroom, showered. Entertaining Caroline was the last thing on earth she wanted to do. Tom's mother she may be, but the woman was a dragon. A dragon with pearls and a twinset. She'd only met Caroline half a dozen times, and that was six times too many.

"Your mother is here. I better go shower and get dressed. I'm sure she was less than impressed to see me waltzing around your kitchen in my robe."

"I don't care what she thinks, Elizabeth." He reached for her, wrapping his arms around her waist. "And you're not getting away from me without a good morning kiss." His eyes held hers a moment, an odd look in them before he lowered his head until their mouths met, taking his time to kiss her thoroughly before he released her.

She reached up for another quick one before she let him go. "Hmmm, I like your good morning kisses."

His eyes turned devilish. "Stand there much longer looking at me like that and you'll get a lot more than just a kiss, sweetheart."

She laughed softly and turned away, warmth filling her. "You can't. Mom's waiting, remember?" she said, rolling her eyes at him before she scampered away, giggling as a hand swatted at her bottom.

"Don't remind me. Now scoot. Before I forget about my mother and fuck that saucy little ass you keep teasing me with."

She peeked out the door to make sure Caroline wasn't around before she ducked around the corner into the guest room.

TAKING AS LONG AS she dared, Elizabeth turned off the shower, toweling the excess water from her hair before running a comb through it and leaving the steamy bathroom.

Opting for a pair of jeans and a sweatshirt, not wishing to aggravate Caroline any more than necessary by swanning around in her robe, she took one final look at herself in the mirror before she planted a smile on her face and walked out of her room.

She refused to let Caroline spoil her happy mood. Tom loved her. He hadn't stopped loving her, and she loved him.

They were both older now. Wiser. They could work out their problems.

They could work out any—

She stopped as she rounded the corner to the kitchen. Tom's words halting her in her tracks.

". . . and I don't care what you think it looks like, Mother. Elizabeth is my model . . ."

Pain hit Elizabeth like a sledgehammer. Memories of that day two years ago. The words the same. The situation a mirror of the day he'd denied her, denied them, and broken her heart.

Her fragile little bubble of happiness popped as she saw Tom looking at her, a pained expression on his face.

No, not again. No! She couldn't stand it. Her breath locked in her throat and she tried to tell her feet to move. To get out of there. He was going to do it again, and she didn't think her heart could take it twice.

Tears filled her eyes, the pounding in her ears blocking out whatever Caroline was saying. She could see Tom's mouth moving as he watched her, but no sound was getting through.

And she didn't want to hear. She didn't want to know.

All she wanted was to leave. Run.

But Tom was walking toward her. His dark eyes holding hers, his expression angry.

Finally getting her feet to move, she took a step back as he reached for her. But his hold on her wrist was firm, halting her escape.

"Elizabeth. Don't." Though his expression was dark and she could feel the anger pouring out of him, his words were surprisingly gentle. "Come here, sweetheart."

She shook her head frantically. *Why?* she wanted to ask. *So you can destroy me again?*

As he pulled her against him, his head lowered until his lips brushed against hers, and she closed her eyes as a couple of tears breached the lids, followed by another and another.

And then he straightened, still holding her, and faced his mother.

"The family, the great Danville line," he said mockingly, "can all go get stuffed, Mother."

Elizabeth flinched at Caroline's shuddering indrawn gasp, the look of pure venom on his mother's face as she locked onto her.

"Along with all those vapid, dimwitted, supposedly 'suitable' young ladies you keep throwing at me," Tom continued.

A finger under Elizabeth's chin turned her face until she could look at him, see the smile in his eyes as he looked down at her.

"I'm marrying Elizabeth, if she'll have me after the total bastard I've been to her."

"But you can't!" insisted Caroline in the background. "When your father goes, you'll inherit the title. You'll be Lord Danville." Her tone turned cajoling. "You need someone who will be an asset to you, darling, who can help you, who knows how to act, how to dress . . ." She looked down her nose at Elizabeth and her tone sharpened. "Not some . . . some cheap—"

"Enough!" Tom's roar was so loud it made Elizabeth jerk in his arms. "Don't you ever, *ever*, dare speak to or about Elizabeth that way," he growled.

"But—"

"What I need," he bit out, cutting his mother off as he continued to glare at her, "is someone who loves me. *Me*, plain old Tom.

Not the heir to the fucking Danville fortune."

"Thomas!" Caroline gasped in shock.

"I *need*," he gritted out, trying to bring his anger under control, "the woman I love, Mother. The woman I've always loved. And if you and the family don't like it, you can go and get f—"

Elizabeth reached up quickly to cover his mouth with her fingertips, stopping him from committing a bigger sin than he already had. He looked down at her and she smiled up at him. "I've told you before about saying that, Tom. Besides, I think that's enough bad language out of you for one day," she said and winked. "And yes," she said softly, "I'll marry you."

"Thank heavens for that."

"You'll be sorry, Thomas. Mark my words, this girl will bring you nothing but grief."

Without taking his eyes from Elizabeth, he answered Caroline. "No, Mother, that's where you're dead wrong." He smiled at Elizabeth, the unmistakable sight of his love for her shining in his eyes, making her heart flutter. "She'll bring me nothing but happiness."

He kept holding her until they heard the lift door slam shut as Caroline stormed out, then kissed her. A slow, heady kiss. Lingering. Gentle. Dancing over her lips, his touch so tender, so full of love, it made her heart clench.

"You're sure, Tom?" she asked moments later when the need for air forced them apart. "I don't want you to be sorry later."

"The only thing I'm sorry about, sweetheart, is that I didn't tell her—and you—two years ago." He kissed her again. "And I don't ever want to see that hurt look in your eyes again, knowing that I put it there. I love you, Elizabeth. And I will always love you."

• • •

So . . . ABOUT THESE PAINTINGS . . ." Elizabeth asked later as she lay
back in the Jacuzzi while Tom sat opposite her, massaging her feet.

"Hmmm? What about them?" With a devilish look, he lifted
one foot to nibble on a toe, the tickling causing Elizabeth to gig-
gle and squirm.

"They're not finished, Tom."

"No. Are you suggesting we do that now?" He ran his hand
from her foot up her inner leg, teasing the lips of her pussy so
that she was soon squirming for an entirely different reason. "I
was really hoping we could find something just as . . . *creative*, to
amuse ourselves. I'm feeling particularly inspired right now . . ."

"Do you think we should get Richard back to pose some
more?" she asked innocently.

Tom's fingers stopped and looked over at Elizabeth.

"No. I don't," he replied, his words slow and distinct.

"But I'm sure there are a few poses we haven't tr—"

Elizabeth's words were cut off as a sharp tug on her feet pulled
her under the bubbling water.

As Tom grasped her around the waist, she came up spluttering
and laughing, water dripping from her lashes, her waist-length
hair streaming behind her to float in the water. He pulled her
flush up against him.

"Minx."

"But darling . . ." she teased.

"Trust me, I've seen enough of Richard's bare butt to last me a
lifetime. I'll do the rest from memory."

"And what about me?" She leaned toward him to kiss him, draping her arms around his neck as she floated fully onto his lap, straddling his thighs. She gasped as he thrust up and slid his now erect cock inside her waiting channel. Small grunts of pleasure left her lips as he began to stroke. "Do I . . . get drawn from . . . memory too?"

"Sweetheart, I've been drawing you from memory every day for two years. Never, ever again. Besides . . ." He nibbled a line along her neck, making her wriggle with the pleasure streaking through her. "I have a special idea for a portrait of the future Lady Danville to hang in the family gallery. I was thinking a lovely nude . . ."

"Tom!"

"Hmmm?"

"You wouldn't!"

"Um-hmmm."

EDIBLE DELIGHTS

JAN SPRINGER

ONE

Several days earlier . . .

AX RIVERS COULDN'T STOP inhaling the succulent scent wafting off the lavender-colored
letter that accompanied the large sample of
edible underwear his elderly assistant had placed on his desk
early this morning.

The sweet smell intrigued him. Made his cock stone-hard
while memories of a certain sexy redhead bombarded him. After
all these years apart he still remembered her sparkling blue eyes,
her slender waist, the curve of her wide hips as she bucked against
him and oh those alley-cat screams that made him all hot and
bothered when his partner Nick and he double penetrated her.

At first he was surprised to discover the sample of her edible
underwear on his desk. It wasn't normal for uptight, irritated,
seventy-five-year-old Maybell to bother him with such an intimate
arrangement unless they belonged to an extremely famous designer.

Why the sudden change?

His design and distribution company Impulse only dealt with

veterans in the design industry and Allie Masters had a long way to go before she was a veteran. Small companies owned by sexy redheads who unexpectedly dumped Nick and him in their ménage a trois relationship several years earlier didn't come into the equation.

Come to think of it, why was Allie, owner of Edible Delights, sending him her erotic wear? What was the sexy bitch up to?

He inhaled deeper, allowing the sensual smell to seep farther into his lungs. Those same wild feelings he experienced every time he'd been around Allie surfaced immediately.

It was *her* scent. Intoxicating. Delicious. Fucking addictive.

The throbbing way his cock's blood vessels pumped wicked jolts of hot blood into his shaft could attest to the fact he hadn't lost a smidgen of interest in her. No woman could make him swell this quickly, this painfully.

Only Allie.

Alluring. Sexy. Evasive Allie. The woman who provoked all his carnal senses just by her scent.

She had been his and Nick's assistant. So damned elusive and seemingly businesslike. Until the night the three of them became trapped in the elevator together. The sexual tension sparking between the three of them over the past couple of years exploded that night.

Nick and he took her there. Took turns fucking her hot, curvy body. In the end they double penetrated her.

Fuck! She was so tight with both of them inside her.

So hot. So wild as she stood trapped between them.

He blew out an excited breath and glanced at the address on

the package. He did a double take. It was a California address. Allie's company's name was on it but in the care of Allie's older sister Sindie.

Hmm . . . interesting. Obviously Sindie was up to her match-making playtime now that Allie had returned from her stay in Europe. Sindie had a knack for matching up lovers at the right time and it was odd that she wasn't attached.

Max found himself smiling despite the uncomfortable way his cock throbbed. Okay, he would play along with Sindie. It was high time Nick and he got Allie back. Then they could all move back in together again and continue the hottest, most satisfying relationship he'd ever been in.

Slamming a finger onto a speakerphone button, he waited anxiously for his elderly assistant to answer.

"Yes, sir?" came Maybell's nasally bored tone.

He hired Maybell shortly after Allie had left her position and moved to Europe. Maybell was a snobby, prim and proper elderly grandmother and totally not his cup of tea. But she once worked for the competition and quit mere months before her forced retirement. He heard rumors she had done it to spite her former boss' son. He had recently taken over the company where she'd worked for almost fifty years. The new boss had told her she was being "put out to pasture" and she was too old to know anything about the new fashions.

She proved them wrong by making the jump to Impulse with ease. She brought with her many trade secrets that quickly pushed Impulse to the top in fashionable erotic wear. She also used her contacts to acquire famous, beautiful models to show off Impulse's designs as well as securing choice spots in fashion shows all over the world. With her help they opened their own successful clothing distribution company.

Maybell ran their company with damned accurate efficiency. He knew without a doubt she had brought Impulse to the top of the fashion industry just to spite her old employer. But that didn't matter. Nick and he would be forever grateful for her help.

"Maybell, get a hold of the owner of Edible Delights."

"Edible Delights, sir?"

"The samples you brought in this morning."

"Samples, sir? I didn't— Oh! You mean *those* samples. I noticed they are quite different than what we're used to. Although I'm sure she has her edibles patented, I have contacts who can go around this small-time company. I thought you might want to copy them. Send them to one of our own top designers to duplicate."

Like hell!

"I want a meeting with the owner . . . Allie Masters . . . at Club Rendezvous." Club Rendezvous was a swingers club in Alberta, Canada. A friend of theirs owned it. Allie wouldn't suspect Nick and he were behind the meeting if it took place way up in Canada—that is, she wouldn't suspect until it was too late.

"I want Impulse to try out her European Fling line." That's what Allie was calling her latest line of edibles. "Make it this weekend. Saturday night. Tell her to bring enough sexy edibles to outfit at least two hundred people. She'll be generously compensated."

There was a momentary silence on the other end and he could almost picture Maybell pursing her lips in disappointment. Up until now he always followed her ideas and suggestions because he knew her fifty years of experience was a hell of a lot better than his ten.

"But, sir, I thought it would be better for one of our own experienced designers—"

"Maybell?" he cut her off, suddenly feeling very impatient with her.

"Yes, sir?"

"Don't tell her who Nick and I are. Or the company we represent. Give us a couple of famous names from a top competition company."

"Sir?"

He could hear the utter surprise in her voice. Her curiosity about his steering away from the norm. Maybell had never seen his impulsive side so it was understandable she'd be knocked off kilter and question him.

Allie had always brought out his wild ways. Ways he never even knew he had until the sexy redhead had applied for the assistant position.

The way he reacted to her was another reason he loved her so much. Up until meeting her, he had planned everything in his life around Impulse. Since she left, he returned to that boring routine. Even sex with the handful of casual dates over the years was planned. Planned and boring.

It was time he and his good friend and business partner Nick Edwards showed Allie exactly how much they still missed her and how much they wanted her back.

"Make her an offer she can't refuse. And, Maybell?"

"Yes, sir?"

"Thanks." He cut her off and returned his attention to the elite arrangement of edibles he'd strewn across his desk. The first one that caught his eye was a rose-colored thong with an elegant sparkling of edible pale blue crystal beads that edged the waistband. There were several other items including a skimpy champagne-colored panty and bra set. It was made for a woman who wanted to give the impression she was angelic, a virgin.

Definitely not Allie.

He picked up a red-hot bra and instantly smelled juicy strawberries. Exquisite, delicate red lace edged the sheer see-through cups.

It had been designed for a sexy, daring woman by a sexy daring woman.

Allie.

He let out a tense breath and leaned closer. Stroking his tongue along the middle of the right cup where a tight, hard nipple would have been, he enjoyed the smooth way the material melted onto his tongue. He groaned at the deliciously sweet explosion of strawberry bursting against his taste buds. His eyes widened with surprise as he noted another flavor. Damned if the material didn't have a hint of Italian sweet port wine in it too. Real wine, if he wasn't mistaken.

Fuck.

She'd really learned something working over there in those European fashion companies, hadn't she? She really had known what she wanted when she left their company and headed overseas to be a red-hot designer.

Nick and he had not supported her efforts. Didn't encourage her to pursue her dreams. They were selfish. Wanted her all to themselves. Wanted her to remain their assistant and warming their beds.

Max shook his head and shoved aside the feelings of regret

and guilt. There was no time for regret. No room for guilt. No time to waste.

He wanted Allie back. Knew Nick had never gotten over the ménage a trois relationship they shared either. Truthfully, it had been a bit awkward for all three of them at first, after that night in the elevator. Having sex with Allie and having Nick there watching them and vice versa. But Nick and he admitted to each other they were in love with Allie. They decided the best way to save their close friendship as well as get the woman they both wanted would be a ménage relationship. Thankfully she agreed. Deep down in his gut he knew she was the only woman they would ever share with each other because she was *the one*.

He gave the bra another lick, loving the way the silky material disintegrated in his mouth. He had never tasted anything so good in edible underwear. Hell, it didn't even taste like edible material. It tasted like strawberries and port wine, and not a hint of an aftertaste.

Nope, he had never tasted anything so perfect. Except Allie's hot, pink pussy.

At the memory of how juicy and sweet she tasted, his cock swelled to yet another painful level. This time the sensations felt sharper. Fiercer. He found himself shifting uncomfortably in his chair. Maybe this weekend was going to be too long a wait for him. He looked down and watched the harsh way his pants tented above his erection. He'd waited a long time to react this way to a woman again. Too damned long. Nick and he would make Allie cat's pussy purr and, rest assured, they'd make her think twice about leaving them again.

Two

Several days later . . .

ALLIE MASTERS NERVOUSLY INSPECTED the crisp bouquet of edible undergarments she laid out on the long table. Everything looked perfect. Just like a buffet. From the tasty panties and matching bras flavored to taste like ice wine in a bright watermelon-color to the brown-and-green-colored striped thongs for men tasting of Irish mint chocolate alcohol.

She brought along every savory piece of erotic clothing she had available in the factory on such short notice including her most popular side dishes—Austrian raspberry brandy nipple shields and Swiss chocolate edible condoms.

To tell the truth, she still couldn't believe her luck. The assistant to one of the United States' most popular adult clothing designers had called and asked if she would be interested in presenting a demo of her opening European Fling line.

Hell! Who wouldn't be interested? She said "yes" before she realized she hadn't even targeted that particular company or known the full details of supplying a club full of swingers in Alberta, Canada, as a test for her clothing line.

Later that same day she received a hefty certified check via courier sealing the deal.

Her first instinct had been to decline the offer. She knew the swinging scene would bring up too many memories of her time with Max and Nick. Even now as she thought about her two former bosses and what she experienced with them, she felt so hot she literally had to fan herself with one of the panties she held in her hand.

Sex with Nick and Max had been awesome. She would have stayed with them for the fantastic sex alone but she discovered she wanted more from the three-way relationship. She knew she had their love but she also wanted their support. She hadn't found that support. When she decided to spread her wings and pursue fashion design, Nick and Max had seemed more concerned in keeping her as their assistant and in bed with them rather than helping her achieve her goals. It had been a blow to her self-esteem and to her confidence. Realizing her need for independence, she left Impulse and her two well-hung lovers, accepting a job at a prestigious erotic wear company in Italy. She moved up the ranks, getting jobs in Portugal then ending up in Paris, France before gleaning enough experience to return home and launch Edible Delights.

Business was brisk following her round of fashion shows and now she could barely keep up with supplying her customers her unique designs and erotic-flavored edible fashions. All her hard work and sacrifices had paid off. But now it was time to jump into the big time and she needed a distributor to help.

With her dreams fulfilled she was happy career-wise but unhappy personally. Not to mention she was awfully horny without

Max and Nick. Lately she craved them as never before. She wanted to pick up their relationship but pride kept her in California near her sister Sindie and away from New York City where her two ex-lovers lived and ran their lucrative fashion design and distribution company. The last thing she wanted to do was to go begging for some red-hot sex from the two men she abandoned.

She hadn't even realized what she left behind until she'd been in Europe. She hadn't realized how much she loved the untraditional setup of their ménage a trois relationship either. Two men who adored her so much they willingly shared her. She knew too if they ever forced her to decide between them, she wouldn't be able to. She loved them both dearly.

Max hid his sensuality behind a stern, rigid routine she finally managed to collapse. A man who made her heart skip a beat every time she thought of him.

And Nick whose easygoing attitude and dreamy brown eyes turned her hotter than hell with just one bold "I'm going to fuck you" look.

They were absolutely the perfect combination for her. They were straight men, boyhood friends, who happened to have the same ideas about designing and distributing erotic wear. Men who just happened to fall in love with the same woman.

Her.

She let out a tight breath as she caught her reflection in a nearby mirror. Her shoulder-length wavy red hair glowed brilliantly beneath the overhead lights. She wore little makeup. Just a dusting of gold eye shadow and a zip of pink lipstick.

Tonight she dressed herself in a sexy curve-hugging, gold-colored Gianni Versace viscose-jersey dress with soft fuchsia pantyhose and snappy high-heeled shoes. She wore blue sapphire drop clip-on earrings that highlighted the blue in her eyes and diamond line bracelets that clinked gently every time she moved her arms.

Allowing the zipper of her dress to remain open to mid-breast, she gave everyone a curvy glimpse. She also allowed several necklaces to scatter prettily along her chest area. Necklaces that included a diamond sun medallion pendant and an imitation diamond sautoir necklace. She hadn't wanted to look like the perfect businesswoman but instead opted for a fresh, alive appearance. Someone of confidence. A carefree woman comfortable with her own sexuality.

"Why so glum?" Her older sister Sindie asked as she entered the room with the last box full of edible wear. "You should be ecstatic, woman. Free rein of a swingers club and two top designers who want to sample your stuff. I'd be over the moon, Al. How come you're not?"

"Oh I am happy," Allie replied as she pounded the nervous butterflies back down her throat. She grabbed a handful of clothing. Laying them out on the table, she made sure to put the appropriate note in front of each pile to let the swingers know the name of each item and a warning to beware of alcoholic content in the clothing.

"You don't sound it, sweetie." Sindie frowned as she lifted a bundle of Spanish mango champagne-striped panties. She settled them between the almond-colored Italian Assassin–flavored and the buttery yellow-colored Italian Limoncilla–flavored outfits.

"Okay, so I'm nervous as hell," Allie admitted. "This is probably a once-in-a-lifetime chance. If these Nico and Leo guys don't like my designs and decide not to distribute my lines, that's it, game over. I may as well just stay small-time."

"First of all, you aren't even small-time. You can barely keep up with the orders. Second, you already have a second factory waiting to prepare upcoming orders and third—trust me—these guys will love you and they'll love your designs. No one can deny an Edible Delights erotic wear."

"I wish I had your confidence, sis."

"That's why you asked me to come along." Sindie wiggled her eyebrows. "Because I inject confidence. What else are sisters for? And it's perfectly normal for you to be nervous. This is something big and exciting."

"I just don't understand why you went behind my back and sent that company my samples? They're one of the top distributors. They shouldn't be giving me the time of day."

"Because you are one of the top, that's why."

"They could easily have had someone duplicate my designs. I would have been knocked out of business."

Sindie laughed. "That's what they have patents for. And yours are all up to date. Besides, you should have an agent to represent your stuff. I've told you that so many times. But just don't worry. The big guys want to look at your wear in action. That says something." Her sister winked. "And you can do a little swinging on the side just like I'm going to do tonight. No-strings sex is right up my alley. And I'm going to have fun showing off your French Stinger lingerie and have even more fun when my catch of the night nibbles it off my body."

Allie felt herself flush. "Like I said, I wish I had your confidence."

Sindie had loads of confidence. She was a beautiful woman, five years Allie's senior. Tonight she wore a gorgeous baby blue slinky tube dress with a cutout front area that showed off her gold belly ring. With mid-back-length auburn hair and glittering hazel eyes, not to mention a gorgeous body that most women would die for, her sister looked like a top fashion model and Allie had used her quite often for her fashion shows.

With an extremely profitable wedding planner business, several employees working for her and lots of friends who adored her, Sindie appeared to have it made. But her sister was also one of those women who played matchmaker to everyone and ended up the bridesmaid and never the bride at those friends' weddings. Allie hoped her sister's luck would change. She hoped her own luck would change too. Since leaving Max and Nick she was spoiled from ever having a normal relationship with just one man. In Europe she went out with several men and dabbled in sex. She always compared them to Nick and Max. Those European men had always come up short, in more ways than one.

Dammit! Would she ever get over Max and Nick?

She would have to try. Tonight after her business meeting. She would play with the swingers. Have some wild, hot, no-strings sex. It would be her "coming out" party. Or if she were lucky, it would be a sex party to celebrate a business venture with the two designers who were so interested in distributing her European Fling line.

"There, that's better," Sindie giggled. "It looks as if you're starting to be happy. Hold that thought and that smile, little sister. It's time to party!" She grabbed Allie's hand, pulling her away from the buffet of clothing and toward the door.

The minute they erupted into the stairwell, Allie's heart began a frantic pound. The music sounded wild and loud as it drifted from below. Several men and women were already heading up the narrow staircase. The men's eyes glittered with lust as they eyed Sindie and Allie.

Allie's pulse pounded erratically as one of the men, a very Italian-looking hottie of maybe ten years her junior, rubbed his thick erection against her thigh as he squeezed past.

As the swollen flesh pushed against her, she found herself shivering with both nerves and excitement.

"You two. Upstairs. I'm hot tonight," he said softly, and stopped on a stair above them.

"She's taken, stallion," Sindie laughed, and pulled Allie along farther down the stairs.

"Maybe later, gorgeous ladies?" the man purred after them.

"Sure, later. It's a date," Allie called out to him, and couldn't believe what she just said.

"Wowsa, woman. You're getting into this fast. But first you need to meet these distributors. Remember? The business meeting? Come on. The private dining areas are back here."

She was pulled through an almost dark room jam-packed with dancers. The hordes of men and women danced erotically to a pounding beat of wild ear-splitting music. It was hot in the room. Hot and wild. She could literally feel the music sift into her body. Could feel herself begin to gyrate and hum.

The magic was broken as a moment later they pushed past a thick set of doors and entered another hallway.

At least it was a little quieter. Quiet and totally deserted.

"Here, Dining Room Number Seven. This is your room. Go on in. I'll see if I can't find them."

Before Allie could stop Sindie and remind her that the distributors might already be inside, she had swept down the hallway leaving her alone. The rush of nerves hit her again as she stared at the closed door.

She thought about taking off. Of pretending these two men weren't going to show. She could melt back into her little business. Back to the status quo. But she didn't want the status quo. She wanted full distribution like the big guys. She wanted to be with the big guys. She wanted recognition for her hard work. Recognition and a good sexual release.

The last thought made her flush. Then reality bit into her again.

Business first. Playtime later.

Taking a deep breath she summoned the nerve to knock, waited a moment and then opened the door.

She stepped inside. And froze.

Two men sat at the table reading menus. When they looked up and saw her, lust shone brightly in a pair of glittering blue eyes and a pair of breathtaking brown eyes.

Fuck! Her knees almost melted at the intoxicating way they gazed at her.

"Hello, Allie cat," Max's deep voice sparkled along her nerve endings bringing a long forgotten warmth shooting into her body. Max was the spitting image of Richard Gere. With gorgeous white teeth as he smiled at her, a light dusting of silver stranding through his black hair, he looked absolutely stunning wearing a black tuxedo and crisp vanilla-colored shirt with a sprig of white freesia peeking out from the breast pocket.

"Long time no see, kitten," Nick, the younger of the two partners, added. He also wore a black tuxedo with a shimmering white shirt. A striking red rose was stuck in the breast pocket.

As he placed the menu back on the table, he studied her boldly. Nick wasn't as shy as Max and he looked as gorgeous as ever. He wore his golden brown hair shoulder-length and always had a sexy five o'clock shadow. Her pussy creamed as she remembered how erotic that beard felt brushing against her sensitive inner legs all those times he went down on her.

"What are you two doing here?" She could barely talk, her voice coming out in a breathy, sexy whisper.

"Having a meeting," Max replied casually.

"Oh I must have the wrong room."

She felt flustered. Too stunned to move. Too surprised to even formulate a thought.

She should leave but all she could do was stare at the two men who'd captured her heart several years ago.

"Since you appear to be staying, let's have a drink for old times' sake," Max said as he grabbed a bottle of wine chilling in a nearby crystal bucket.

"Yes, come on, kitten. Join us," Nick drawled.

Shit. She needed to leave. Needed to think.

"I . . . have a meeting." Yeah, that's it. She had a meeting. A very important meeting. "I must have made a mistake about the room."

"Oh there's no mistake, kitten." Nick smiled. "If you're looking for Nico and Leo, you've found us."

What?

Max poured the wine into three goblets and held one up to her. "Cheers to your sister for bringing us together again."

Disappointment rolled through Allie in one horrible wave. "My sister?"

"She set it up for us to meet," Nick said smoothly.

Her stomach plummeted in disappointment. God! How cruel of them to get her hopes up like this. What in the world had Sindie been thinking?

A sudden burst of tears bit the back of her eyes and damned if they were going to see her cry.

"I'm outta here," she said quickly. Turning on her heel, she headed for the door.

God! She had worked so hard to get tonight together. Had her hopes pinned on this meeting. Until now she had no idea how high those hopes had been. Sparing no expense, she had persuaded her workers into overtime to produce more garments at such short notice. Some of them had given up valuable family time during evenings to help her out. Obviously it had been all for nothing.

"It was my idea for you not to know. I was afraid you wouldn't come." Max's soft voice stopped her at the door.

THREE

*N*ICK BROKE IN QUICKLY, obviously noting her distress. "There really is a business meeting. We wanted to talk to you about your . . . edibles."

The strangled way he said "edibles" made her think he was talking about more than just her clothing line. Despite the devastation, she felt her face heat as she remembered exactly how good his tongue felt when he tongue-fucked her.

"Don't look so disappointed, Allie," Nick soothed. "We're extremely interested in seeing what you have to offer after your European fling."

She stiffened at his remark and turned to face the bastards.

"Fling?" The familiar anger burst from inside her. The sons of bitches had never taken her seriously when she informed them she wanted to become a designer instead of just their assistant. Why in the world did she still care what they thought anyway? She knew she shouldn't give a rat's ass about their opinions, but she did.

"Isn't that what you're calling your new line?" Nick said coolly. "European Fling. Edible underwear with a European taste. Love the hint of alcohol in the material by the way."

"There is no business meeting between us. I can make Edible Delights big on my own. I don't need your help."

"Ah yes, the ever independent woman. It's one of the reasons we were so attracted to you, kitten," Nick answered softly.

Were? As in past tense. A painful spear of hurt ripped through her. They considered her their past, just as she should be considering them her past.

"We've upset you. Please, sit down, cat." Max lifted one of the wine goblets and held it out to her while taking a sip from his own then smacking his luscious lips, groaning his appreciation. "We truly want to talk about your edibles. What have you got to lose?"

My heart, dammit! She wanted to say. Even though they didn't support her dreams, she still wanted to have them in her life. Other than not being behind her career choice, they had been so attentive to her emotional needs and sexual cravings. She always felt loved by them and never regretted living with the two of them.

Although they may consider her a part of their past, Max's blue eyes glittered with the same intense interest he always looked at her with. And she could read the same amusing glint in Nick's brown eyes that had always been there for her. She found herself marveling again at how these two men were a perfect combination. Max, ever-so serious, planned his every minute of the day, while Nick, his total opposite, had no schedule and just simply flew by the seat of his pants. But together they made the perfect team, owning an extremely successful distribution line of erotic wear as well as designing men's and women's erotic clothing with such intricate care they were the envy of competing designers.

And she fell into the envy trap too. Wanted to be just like them. Wanted to be their equal in every way. Was that such a bad thing to strive for?

"Don't let our rift screw your future for Edible Delights. You've got a winner on your hands," Nick said coolly as Max continued to hold out the wine goblet for her.

She snatched the goblet away and sat down on the empty chair. Holding Nick's gaze, she felt a burst of boldness and immense pride at her accomplishments as she stared him down. Sure, she knew she shouldn't base her self-worth on what other people thought of her, but this was Nick. He was a man she lived with for several years. A man who fucked her daily. He loved to tease her and please her. He was a weakness of hers and it felt good to be acknowledged by him.

She took a big swig of the sweet wine, marveling at the sweet explosion against her taste buds. Max always had damned good taste in wine and by the soft way he was smiling at her, she knew he was just as proud of her as Nick.

Her earlier disappointment at being duped was disintegrating fast. If it were a business meeting they wanted, they'd soon realize she wasn't so easily pushed around.

"You're damn right I have a winner, Nick," she said firmly.

She watched with smug satisfaction as a look of surprise washed over his face. She wasn't one for accepting compliments easily and it was obvious he hadn't expected her to agree. In the past she would have fluttered and gushed like a teenager but now she was prepared to fight to expand her company.

"Looks like our kitten has grown claws," Nick teased, and guzzled back some wine.

Allie found herself gazing around at her environment for the first time. The tablecloth looked exquisite in a solid coral shade with a cream-colored embroidered overlay. An arrangement of gorgeous white flowers—dahlias, tulips, snapdragons and clustered hydrangeas sat in a clear glass container in the middle of the table. A pang of nostalgia hit as she remembered receiving a similar bouquet of flowers the morning after the fantastic night they'd spent fucking her in the elevator when it had stalled between floors.

She inhaled quickly as she remembered their guttural grunts, the sharp slap of flesh against flesh. Could still remember how hot it felt to be sandwiched between their hard masculine bodies. Her yowls during climaxes and mews while being aroused had earned her the nickname of "cat" from Max and "kitten" from Nick.

"No, this is no business meeting," she found herself whispering. It was a setup to take her down memory lane.

"Your face is starting to flush," Max said in a hoarse voice.

Despite the heat enveloping her, Allie forced herself to meet Max's eyes. "I'm sorry, but it won't work, gentlemen. I won't be seduced by either of you tonight or any night." Hell, the last thing she wanted to do was play easy. Oh she wanted them all right, but she wanted them on her terms.

"We've missed you, kitten. We want you back in our lives. Back in our bed. You're the only woman who makes us feel alive and loved." Nick's admission had her blinking in surprise. He usually made a point in a teasing way, not at all serious as he was suddenly being now. And the way he was looking at her with deliberate seriousness had her breath catching.

"You've taught us a valuable lesson, cat," Max said. "We won't forget it. We realize we can't live without you. Obviously we didn't appreciate you as a whole woman. A woman with dreams and goals. We were selfish. Infatuated with the fantastic sex and not willing to realize you had other needs as well."

"You've got that right," she said coolly. Inside however, she was burning up with excitement. Her two men still wanted her, even after all this time apart.

"We should have come after you, Allie," Nick said. "But we were stubborn. Later we realized you needed your space to grow into the independent woman you wanted to be. We would just have been in the way."

"Hmm, that's nice of you two to admit, gentlemen." She managed to continue to keep her voice calm and businesslike, although inside she was crying with a giddy immature happiness. They missed her just as much as she missed them.

Suddenly both men were standing.

Mercy! She'd forgotten how tall they both were and—

"Oh my God," she found herself whispering as a wave of erotic shock rolled over her.

Neither man wore pants! Nor underwear. Just their tuxedo jackets, white shirts and impressive solid erections.

A split second later her surprise wore off and she shifted uncomfortably as the familiar hot flush of sexual awareness raced through her.

"Um," she found herself saying as she nervously licked her suddenly dry lips, quite unable to keep her eyes from going from one luscious cock to the other.

"Wh-what's gotten into you two?" Like, duh! As if she didn't know.

They'd shared many a business meeting having sex. She shouldn't be so surprised. But she was.

At her question, Nick's lips pursed into an amused pout. Max's eyes blazed with a rush of intense need. Both men watched her as they began stroking their long, thick cocks.

She became all too aware of how wet and pleading her pussy had suddenly become. How intensely hard her breasts were pushing against her jersey dress.

As they touched themselves, both men came toward her from her right. She could literally see the web of veins throbbing in Max's huge, flushed penis. His plum-shaped cock head had already burst free from its sheath. Her fingers clenched as she remembered how heavy and silky his two swollen balls would feel in the palms of her hands. And Nick's cock, her heart fluttered wildly, his cock was just a little thicker and longer than Max's. One lone blue vein ran along his entire shaft topped perfectly with a huge mushroom-shaped head shaded purple.

She blew out a slow breath remembering both men were well over eight inches long and three inches thick.

"As you can see, we've missed you, cat," Max said. His voice sounded strangled and aroused.

"Missed you is quite the understatement," Nick hissed. "Get down on your knees, kitten."

His commanding voice intoxicated her.

Ah shit, she thought as her self-control disintegrated and she found herself going down on her knees before the two.

Reaching out, she grabbed Max's swollen balls and opened her mouth for Nick.

Nick's thick cock head came quickly inside. Hard, needy and hot, it pulsed against her lips.

Both Max and Nick groaned at the same time. The guttural sounds were like music to her ears.

Oh she missed this so much. Missed touching them. Tasting them. Fucking them.

The heat of Max's scrotum laced her palms and she began a hard, sensual massage just the way she knew he liked it. Tightening her lips around Nick's shaft, she felt the lone vein pulse against her tongue. The long, thick shaft sunk into her, his mushroom-shaped cock head tickled the back of her throat. He quickly withdrew and then came into her again.

"We want to hire you to run Impulse's edible line," Nick growled. "You'll have full control over the division. Full creative access. Full hiring capabilities. The works. You'll be the boss of Edible Delights as well. But we want exclusive rights to your edibles and to have the trade secrets you've acquired under the protection of our company."

"In other words," Max growled as she continued her massage, not quite believing what she was hearing.

"We want you as a full partner in the business," Max finished.

Allie was stunned. Both at the way her body responded so brilliantly to their moans of arousal and at their proposition. She would be their equal. Their partner. It was something she had only hoped for in her wildest dreams. Not to mention having full access to her two lovers again.

It would be a perfect union. Something she wanted. She would have an even wider access to suppliers.

She stopped massaging Max's balls and let go of Nick's penis with a pop.

"I'm already the boss of Edible Delights," she whispered hoarsely. "I won't deny my current clients. You can't have exclusive rights but you can have subsidiary rights."

She opened her mouth and Nick slipped in again. She restarted her massaging of Max's hot flesh.

"Fuck," Max moaned.

"Jesus," Nick whispered as she raked her teeth along his rigid shaft.

She loved the way it jerked in her mouth. Loved the hot brand of Max's swollen spheres in her palms, but she had another delicate area to tend to. She let go and grabbed the base of Max's shaft with both hands. Velvety heat licked her fingers as she began a gentle twisting motion she knew he loved.

"You're a shrewd . . . business . . . woman," Max gasped.

In answer she gave his cock an extra hard twist.

"Ouch," he hissed, grabbing her wrists, stopping her cold. "I think I understand. We better be good to you."

She winked at him, signaling he understood her point perfectly. She devoured Nick's cock, taking it deeper into her mouth, allowing his hard velvety flesh to come down into her throat. He slid his fingers through her hair, holding her head, forcing her to look up and meet his intense gaze.

Max let go of her wrists and she could hear the zipper on the front of her dress lowering past her breasts. He pulled aside the cloth and warm air brushed against her flesh. Although Nick's cock impaled her mouth and she couldn't see what Max could see, she noticed his eyes glaze over and knew immediately he liked the bra she wore beneath.

She had picked the cream-colored, strawberry-champagne-flavored one. One of her latest creations using her softest material to date. She watched him lick his full lips. Nice and slow as he studied her heaving breasts. She knew what he wanted to do and she could feel the sexual haze begin to intoxicate her business smarts.

Bastards. They weren't going to seduce her into getting anything less than what she wanted.

"What are your demands, Allie cat?" Max asked.

Nick slid out of her mouth allowing her to answer.

"Edible Delights remains as is. Under my full control," she said, sucking in some needed breaths during the break.

Edible Delights was her baby. Hers alone. Was it wrong not to share it with the two men she loved? *No,* an inner voice answered. *It isn't wrong. It's a sweet deal but the company is your dream. Hold on tight to her. You made her.*

"As I said, I'll grant Impulse subsidiary rights. But for certain future lines that I decide to design for Impulse. And of course I want Edible Delights to get full distribution with Impulse's lines."

"We deal only with exclusive rights, Allie cat. You know that," Max growled. Despite the serious way he spoke, he licked his lips again and lowered his mouth over her right nipple. Heat and moisture seared through her tender flesh and she could literally feel the cloth disintegrate. Pleasure-pain burst through her nipple as his sharp teeth began a rough nibble.

In answer, she grabbed a hold of Max's balls and ran her sharp fingernails along the bottom of his sac.

"You're a fucking tease," he mumbled, and let go of her aching nipple. But she knew he enjoyed the pleasure-pain she inflicted. He looked up at Nick who nodded and traced his swollen cock head as if it were lipstick along the contours of her lips.

"Okay, you win," Max grumbled. "We'll have the lawyers draw up the details and they'll contact you. I'll have our purchasing department contact you first thing when we're finished. We'll send a hefty advance so you can prepare for the order."

Fuck! She's done it! Woo Hoo!

"It's been nice doing business with you, gentlemen."

She opened her mouth and allowed Nick's hot cock back inside. In turn Max began a wild suckle at her breast, making her gasp at the wicked intensity.

NICK COULDN'T BELIEVE HOW the vixen kitten had been able to get what she wanted so easily. He promised himself he would tease her for as long as possible, but one look at the disappointment crushing her face at having been duped and one second of having her lush mouth latch around his cock, she literally sucked all business sense out of him.

He loved Allie.

She made him hot. Made him feel protective of her, teasingly loving and just plain happy. She had him from the moment Max and he interviewed her for the job as their personal assistant.

A young woman. Full of ambition and so sensual. He found himself masturbating to her resume photo right there in his office. He'd masturbated since she left for Europe too.

Sweet shit! All the years they lost. But the three of them

needed the separation. He knew that now. She needed to grow and Max and he needed to grow up.

It had been hard to move out of Max's place after she'd left and try to move on without her. Fucking hard not to go to Europe and yank her onto the first plane back to New York. But now she was back. She would run her own company within Impulse's protection and she would be their partner in every sense of the word.

His erection throbbed as he looked down at her. Necklaces glittered across her perfectly shaped chest, pretty pink lips were stretched around his cock and she stopped her ministrations. Her blue eyes were glazed and she mewed those cute kitty sounds as Max's mouth sucked on her full breast.

"Jesus," he found himself muttering at the erotic sight of another man at her breast. He knew a normal man might be jealous. He wasn't. Not where Max and Allie were concerned. He trusted the two of them so implicitly that sometimes it hurt.

He watched Allie's cheeks flush a deeper red as she caught his gaze. Her blue eyes grew darker and her chest heaved harder.

Oh yes, she missed this too.

He pulled his cock from her tight mouth and pushed into her again, loving the sensual way her smooth lips moved over every sparking nerve ending.

She mewed sweetly again and he lost himself. Circling his fingers around the area of his shaft to where he knew she could take his penis into her, he began a barely controlled thrust in and out of her voluptuous mouth. He closed his eyes and shuddered as an orgasm quickly snowballed.

He thrust once. Twice. Three times. Then his entire body

tightened into an erotic ball of pleasure. White-hot blades of arousal licked his scrotum and seared straight up into his shaft.

He exploded on a strangled shout, spurting into her throat and loving the way her muscles contracted as she eagerly swallowed his seed.

Ah, yes. She hadn't lost her sensual touch. Not by a long shot.

"FUCK! YOU'RE SO DAMNED beautiful," Nick said a few minutes later as he reached down and with a linen napkin dabbed at the semen drooling from Allie's mouth. Having her on her knees before him made him feel fantastic. Having her pink lips wrapped tightly around his shaft, her warm tongue sliding along his sensitive flesh once again was unbelievably great. Even watching Max sucking on her nipples created an erotic sight that aroused him to new heights.

He had dreamed of this day for so long. Now it was finally happening. He could see the lust glowing bright in her eyes. The need for pleasure. The craving to be fucked again by her two lovers.

"Get dressed, kitten," he said.

"Where are we going?" she asked breathlessly.

"Phase two of our business meeting."

And he could barely wait.

FOUR

ALLIE WATCHED WITH GROWING excitement as women giggled and men grinned while they browsed the edible underwear her sister and she had laid out on the table earlier.

As she watched, she tried to ignore the strong, demanding masculine scents of the two men who flanked her. Not to mention she found it hard to overlook the throbbing of her aching breasts where Max had suckled. As well as the intense way her weeping pussy demanded to be filled.

Not even half an hour had gone by since she left this second floor room. Most of the garments were gone and there was still a lineup of swingers eagerly waiting to get something edible to wear. She noted all her business cards were gone too.

A shot of nervousness coursed through her.

"I didn't bring enough for everyone. I'm so sorry," she whispered anxiously.

"You're a hit, cat. We knew you would be," Max said softly against her right ear where he began a bold nibble on her neck behind her earlobe, which sent wickedly delicious shivers racing through her.

"I can go back to my hotel suite and get more," she said in a rush. There were no more edibles back at their hotel. Sindie and she had brought everything with them in their rental van, but it would be a good excuse to leave and gather her bearings. To try to establish some semblance of self-control. She knew they were in the process of successfully seducing her. Knew it was a matter of time before she fell completely under their spell. She always felt so sexually helpless around the two men. Had managed to be elusive for a long time, until that night they'd been trapped in the elevator.

That night she acknowledged what she wanted from them. A need to be fucked by her two bosses. They obliged. Tonight they gave her what she wanted again. Equal partnership. The need to be fucked was just as bad as that first time in the elevator.

Maybe she should get out of there before she caved totally. Before it was too late and she lost her heart all over again.

She made a move.

Nick grabbed her hand, stopping her cold. "Uh-uh, you're staying here with us. Our meeting is far from over, kitten."

Max leaned in close to her right ear. "Yeah, cat. We haven't even gotten to the main course yet—you."

Allie shivered as Max once again drew her earlobe into his mouth and nibbled saucily. Nick's hand slid over the curve of her ass making her moan softly as he started a slow massage against one of her cheeks. His fingers dug into her flesh so perfectly that she could barely concentrate on watching the rest of the men and women quickly pick through the remaining underwear before vanishing through a nearby doorway.

When all but a handful of people stood around the tables looking dejected, Max intertwined his hand with hers and Nick took her other hand.

"Let's go find the changing rooms," Max whispered as they brought her to those mysterious doors where the swingers had disappeared. Her heart crashed a mile a minute as both men silently led her down a long hallway. Doors lined each side of the hall and sexual tension wrapped all around her despite the relative quietness.

The silence was a big contrast to the wild music from the floor below. Instead, there were soft giggles from behind closed doors. She swore she could even hear the rustling of clothing as people undressed.

A nearby door opened and several men and women dressed in her sexy edibles pranced proudly down the hallway toward them.

One of them was her sister!

And she was with the man who hit on them earlier. The Italian stallion.

He wore a skimpy red, strawberry and sherry-flavored thong that enhanced a most impressive package. Allie shivered wonderfully as she spied the vivid outline of his long, thick cock pressing boldly against the material and the two perfectly shaped balls begging to be fondled by a woman's hands.

"Remind me to kill you tomorrow, sis," Allie said when she'd sufficiently recovered from ogling the stallion.

Sindie smiled prettily, cocked an eyebrow at her, then grinned at Max and then at Nick.

"Oh? And would that be before or after you thank me?"

"How's about that date you promised me earlier? You join us, sexy lady," the stallion interrupted. His eyes were heavy-lidded with wanting and Allie's breath caught as she imagined having sex with this man and her sister.

"I've never had the privilege of pleasuring two sisters at the same time."

"Easy, stallion. Those two are her men," Sindie replied. "They don't share with anyone but each other. Besides, you'll have your hands quite full with me."

The man's gaze narrowed as he casually inspected Nick and then Max, who now wore their entire tuxedo outfits, if not a bit rumpled. "You two are a bit overdressed, aren't you?"

"And you're not underdressed?" Nick said coolly, eyeing the stallion's erotic attire.

Allie stifled a laugh. She sensed the hostility seething beneath Nick's calm exterior.

"She's off limits to you tonight, studly," Max said just as coolly.

"Another time then." The stallion looked hopeful as he winked at Allie before her sister tugged him along with her down the hall.

When the three of them were alone again, she noted the tension in both men as they continued to watch the door where the stallion had disappeared with her sister.

"Hey, feel free to join them," she teased, knowing they were more concerned about Sindie like big brothers than lovers.

Both men turned to her and Max replied huskily, "I guess we should have left it up to you if you wanted to join them. Old habits die hard. This is a swingers club and you're free to do what you want."

Nick's gaze narrowed as he watched her closely for an answer.

He'd never been much for sharing her with anyone else but Max so she knew he must be seething.

"I'd rather hang out with you two," she said truthfully. "I'm curious as to what else you've got in store for our business meeting."

"Curious, are you?" Max winked.

"I must admit I have enjoyed it so far."

"By all means then, let's continue," Nick said. From his breast pocket he drew a glistening gold key and inserted it into the door. When it opened, he bowed to Allie as if he were a prince and she a princess. She couldn't help but feel all bubbly and warm that Nick was acting so chivalrous. It was quite out of character for him.

"Your clothing awaits, my lady," he grinned.

She stepped into what appeared to be a large bedroom-sized changing room.

The two men crowded in around the open doorway. Both their faces were flushed with excitement. The hot looks literally made her tremble with anticipation.

"Meet us in Room Three. One floor up, after you get dressed," Max whispered. "And we will make all your wishes come true."

The door closed and she was alone, surrounded with a vista of mirror-tiled walls. She caught the flushed redness of her cheeks, the windblown appearance of her red hair and her lips, full and swollen after sucking off Nick.

Tonight had turned into anything but the business meeting she anticipated. While negotiating with her ex-lovers she had sucked one of them off and had her nipples tended to by the other. And now she was in a changing room ready to have sex with them after all these years of being apart.

And she could hardly wait to be impaled by them. Just as she had barely been able to wait to have both of them inside her the night they'd become trapped in the elevator.

God! It felt as if it were only yesterday . . .

"WE'RE TRAPPED," ALLIE SIGHED as she finally gave up on pressing the red emergency button on the elevator panel and slumped heavily against the nearby steel wall. The elevator had come to a grinding halt a good ten minutes ago. There was no phone to call for help but surely at this late hour someone would eventually notice that it hadn't arrived at the first floor?

"Don't sound so down about it, Allie, I'm sure we can find something to do to amuse ourselves until the morning," Max said softly from beside her.

Her pulse picked up a wild speed as she looked up to find him watching her. Lust shone brightly in his blue eyes and she felt her heart flutter as it always did when she looked at him.

Oh boy. This was not good. She could not spend too much time in here with these two gorgeously sexy men. Since becoming their assistant, she tried like hell to remain aloof and professional around them but it was getting harder and harder. Especially in the almost overwhelming sexual way she felt attracted to both of them.

"That's right, sweet lady. We've got all night," Nick whispered in a strangled breath.

"All night? Surely there's someone around?" She tried hard to ignore the wicked way her pulse was picking up speed at the thought of being alone with Max and Nick all night.

"We're the only ones left in the building. Remember?" Max said in a tight voice. "Today was a holiday. No one is coming until the morning."

Her gaze snapped to Nick, who suddenly seemed closer to her. Actually both men seemed rather closer.

Oh boy. It sure was getting hot in here.

"I think it's time we show her exactly how we feel about her. Don't you think, Nick?"

"Yes, we've been discussing you behind your gorgeous back, Allie," Nick agreed.

They'd been talking about her? She began to feel her face flush with heat.

"We've been talking about how nice it would be to get to know you a hell of a lot better." Max came closer. His dominant scent washed around her and pinned her to the wall. The intoxicating warmth of his body slammed through her thin summer dress and licked flames along her skin.

"We know you want to get to know us a lot better too, Allie. We can see it in the way your nipples peak whenever one of us is around you. Just like they're doing now."

She held her breath as Nick ran a finger down her bare arm. The heat of his touch made her moan softly.

"And the way your eyes sparkle when one of us looks at you," Max commented as he began to unbutton her dress at the collar.

She looked down. Watched in stunned fascination as Max's fingers quickly and efficiently popped the tiny buttons through the buttonholes with his long fingers.

"I . . . I don't do any such thing," she protested, knowing full well she was lying. Even now as Nick's hand slipped beneath her dress, she could feel her vagina cream and her nipples ache and swell in anticipation of their touches. The instant Nick palmed her pussy, she arched herself against him.

"Oh shit," she whispered as she bonded with his touch.

"We want you, Allie," Max growled hoarsely. "We've discussed our attraction to you. Talked about which one of us should pursue you. In the end we decided we both should."

"What . . . what about what I want?" she found herself asking, unable to keep her thoughts straight as Max pushed aside the opening to her dress to expose her bra.

All three of them were breathing heavily now. She could barely concentrate as Nick massaged her pussy with his palm, bringing out a long buried arousal.

"Do you have any lotion in your bag?" Nick asked.

"Lotion?" Confusion zipped through her.

"For later. Are you an anal virgin?"

She found herself shaking at the thought of anal sex and shook her head. She'd tried it with an old boyfriend a few years back and had enjoyed it. She couldn't wait to have Nick and Max taking her there.

"Yes, hand lotion. Yes, in my purse," she replied hoarsely.

"That'll do."

She felt her breasts jiggle and swell as Max undid the front clasp to her bra. A second later her breasts fell free.

"Fuck, you're so yummy-looking." Max grinned. She held her breath as he lowered his head. "I'm a breast man, Allie. And I have to admit you've got the most perfect breasts I've ever seen."

Fire zipped through her as his tongue caressed her nipple.

"We've wanted you for so long," Nick rasped as he got down

on his knees before her. He hoisted her dress up around her waist. She trembled and automatically spread her legs as he lowered her panties and slipped them off.

"She's got a nice, nude pussy, Max. Just as we suspected."

Max made a guttural sound at her breast and just kept on sucking. His other hand cupped her other breast and he began tweaking her nipples until she mewed.

This can't be happening, she found herself thinking as Nick's head lowered to between her legs.

This was the stuff her fantasies about her two bosses were made of. God help her, she cared and loved them dearly. Wanted this so badly.

In order to steady herself, she reached out and grasped Max's broad shoulder with one hand, placing her other hand on the top of Nick's head. It was an awkward position, being pinned to the cool elevator wall with a man sucking at her breast and another man about to go down on her, but it felt so damn good.

So damned right.

It was at that point she knew she could never go back to the way she'd been living. Never go back to avoiding her feelings for them because they'd just told her they wanted her. By her surrendering to them, they knew she wanted them just as badly.

She screeched when Nick's mouth latched on to her pussy and he began a hard, delicious suck that unraveled her.

She could smell her arousal now. A wild scent erupting from a woman who'd been craving these two men to fuck her for far too long.

"Fuck me!" she demanded as her emotions speared to the surface. She felt hot. Her body tight. Every inch of her on fire.

"Oh God, please fuck me!"

A LOW KEENING SOUND unleashing from Allie's throat snapped her from her memory.

Her breathing was rapid. Her body felt tight. So ready to be fucked. Just like she'd been that night.

She blinked wildly as she remembered what had happened between them on the first floor tonight. Moaned softly as she thought of what would happen when she left the security of this changing room.

Could she have sex with them tonight? An inner voice of doubt taunted. Would she lose her independence? Lose sight of her dreams? Would she lose her heart to them all over again?

Ah hell, her heart was already lost to them.

But were Max and Nick truly serious when they said they wanted her back? Would they end up ignoring her dreams again? Would she end up in their bed 24/7 because she simply loved having sex with both of them? But she also enjoyed the independence of running her own company and had grown used to living alone.

Why did life have to be so hard? Why couldn't she just be satisfied with having red-hot sex with the two men she loved tonight and see what happened?

She blew out a tense breath and watched a stray strand of her strawberry red hair flutter around her flushed face.

Yes, she was ready for a good roll with Nick and Max. She would think about other things afterward.

With trembling fingers she unzipped her dress and noticed the melted fabric of her bra around her rosy nipples. The sight of it made her even hornier.

Yes, she wanted sex tonight. Afterward she wanted more than sex from them. Being here with them had dredged up the familiar feelings of frustration again. She knew she should be pushing them aside, but she just couldn't seem to do it. They said they'd learned their lesson. She needed to trust them. Needed to follow her heart.

Her gaze dropped to the bench that extended along one mirrored wall of the changing room. A puffy pink terrycloth robe lay neatly there. She lifted it and spied the gorgeous outfit beneath the robe.

A bra and thong set she designed.

A leopard print dotted with delicate pink rosebuds. She knew the black spots were dark-chocolate-liquor-flavored. The beige-spotted areas were vanilla brandy and the white areas of the print were flavored with white Swiss chocolate. She added the rosebuds for romance and made them strawberry-ice-wine-flavored. This design had been her most challenging to date and her most expensive. She planned to have it in her European Fling line but she hadn't been able to bring herself to duplicate it for anyone.

It was *her*.

Sexy and playful. A sentimental reminder of Nick and Max who enjoyed calling her kitten and cat respectively.

Yes, she would kill Sindie for removing it from her factory. But first she would thank her for reuniting her with her men.

Excitement flared as she removed her jewelry, undressed and

donned the silky bra and thong. The material felt as soft as a flower's petals and smelled delicately delicious.

Allie would cherish tonight. Cherish her memories of whatever developed as a result of making love with her men. If things didn't work out down the line, so be it. She would at least have given their relationship another try. No one died of a broken heart. No one got what she wanted either if she didn't at least give something she wanted badly enough a second chance.

Her breath stalled as she wrapped the toasty pink robe around her and stepped from the changing room. Several men wearing various shades of her edible underwear walked past with a gorgeous brunette.

The woman wore one of Allie's designs. A virgin white panty and bra set flavored in vanilla brandy.

Obviously the men were preparing her for a ménage. Allie's pussy creamed as she watched one of the men wink at Allie before leaning his head down to start licking at the cup on the brunette's right breast. The material quickly dissolved to reveal a plump burgundy nipple. The man moaned in pleasure. Allie imagined how the edible material burst sweetly against his tongue.

She wondered how the woman could even walk with the man nibbling on her nipple the way he did. The other two men were too busy to notice Allie was watching because one had attached his mouth to her earlobe and the other had his fingers inside the woman's ass, plunging in and out in a gentle manner.

Allie swallowed and followed them up the stairs to the third floor. Here the hallway was alive with sounds. Slurping noises. Flesh slapping against flesh. Hushed whimpers and hoarse moans.

Her pussy continued to cream warmly at the erotic sounds

and she moved quickly along the hallway. Through one door she spied a young couple going at it in a doggie position. The woman's mouth was open in a silent scream while the man pummeled her with his huge cock.

Quickly she passed the door and found Room Three. Her legs trembled as she twisted the knob and entered. Nick and Max hadn't arrived yet and she found herself dazzled by the ultra-huge king-sized bed in the middle of the room. It was decked out with plush black satin pillows and leopard print satin sheets that matched the design of the edible clothing she wore.

She smiled warmly.

Bastards. Obviously they'd wasted no time in duplicating her rose leopard design. She should have had it patented. At least then she could have used it to blackmail them into hot sex whenever she wanted it. For a moment she smiled at that thought then frowned as another thought followed. Having that kind of control over her two men would only make things less spontaneous between them.

She looked around the room and didn't miss the racks lining a far wall. Racks containing different sizes of whips, packaged ball gags and other types of bondage gear such as leather restraints and handcuffs.

She wasn't into any of that. Neither were Max and Nick. The three of them had more than enough pleasure without the help of toys.

She noted the scent of freesia in the air and discovered a bundle of white flowers in a nearby crystal vase. A lone white candle flickered in one of the two windows. Her men still had a taste for romance. The thought made her smile.

She jumped as a pair of hot hands curled around her shoulders. Immediately she smelled Max's spicy aftershave and Nick's musky scent. Her senses jolted into awareness mode. Body heat slammed into her, making her nerve endings sparkle with excitement.

"You like?" Nick purred and quickly kissed the sensitive area behind her ear.

"It's gorgeous," she admitted, loving the tingles his kiss created. Loving his hot breath caressing her neck.

"You're gorgeous too, Allie," Max said softly from beside her.

She held her breath as Nick slowly pushed the pink terrycloth robe down her shoulders. The robe didn't have a sash so it quickly dropped off her and puddled around her feet.

She watched Max's eyes widen with appreciation. Then she sighed as Nick's hands cupped her leopard-clad breasts. His palms felt like two white-hot brands, his fingers like fire as he boldly pinched her flesh with expert touches. He had her nipples scorched with pleasure and her moaning within seconds.

"I've missed being with you, kitten. I've missed us," Nick whispered hoarsely.

She found him pressing her forward, toward the bed.

"I have too," she admitted. "More than you know."

"Stand beside the bed, Allie. Bend over, grab the sheets for support. Spread your legs. I need to taste you, bad. I can't wait any longer."

Allie's heart beat wildly. She felt flushed. With fiery excitement she leaned over and took the required position while Max stood by and watched.

Nick's hands were hot as he cradled her ass curves.

"You smell so good, Allie. Such a succulent package."

His hot breath whispered between her legs. She cried out as his mouth nestled between her cheeks. His moist tongue dissolved the fragile material there and he began a mad lick against her labia.

Heat coursed through her pussy. Her fingers wrapped tighter into the leopard satin sheets.

"Oh fuck," she swore as Nick's tongue boldly stroked her clit.

"I can't believe I didn't go after you in Europe, kitten." He lapped harder. The velvety sensations of his tongue between her legs made her pussy clench with wicked anticipation.

"We thought we'd lost you forever," Nick growled. He grabbed her hips, holding her steady. Sharp, sweet pain zipped through her labia as teeth bit her delicate flesh. He rubbed the trapped ends with his tongue and she found herself hissing at the kiss of flames. Found her thighs tightening as his teeth let her pussy lips go and his tongue smoothed over her sensitive clitoris again. He began an erotic circular stroke, the firm pressure making her arch her back, making her mew and whimper for more.

She wanted to tell him he and Max had never lost her. That her heart yearned for both of them, but she couldn't speak from all the pleasure screaming through her. She waited for them to come for her in Europe. She knew that now. Why else had she been unable to start any serious relationships with the men she dated? She wanted to tell Max and Nick all those things but Nick's tongue was now drilling her clit so hard and fast it left her literally panting for air.

Her hips were moving now. Gyrating with need at Nick's every bold stroke against her sensitive flesh. She could feel the heat of her liquid gushing down her vagina toward him. His tongue expertly manipulated her pleasure center until her body ached and she literally felt the inferno of lust raging through her.

"I can see that Allie cat is being nicely primed," Max replied hoarsely as he came into her view. He was undressed and stood in front of her, breathing heavily as he massaged the huge bulge of his erection covered by a skimpy yellow thong.

It was one of her designs. She had to admit it looked very nice on him.

His body looked hard too. Every inch of him a perfect male. His abdomen was rigid and tight. Not an ounce of fat on either of her men.

His muscles were smooth and tanned. She knew they both worked out daily at the company gym. Knew they tanned naked up on Max's penthouse balcony every weekend. At least they had when she lived with them.

God! She couldn't wait to move in with them again. Couldn't wait to start fucking them on the balcony. In the elevator. On the kitchen table. In the whirlpool.

She jerked and moaned as Nick's tongue hit an extra sensitive spot on her engorged clit. It felt three times bigger—swollen and throbbing so hot against Nick's tongue.

Her breaths came faster and faster. The blood in her body heating with passion as she watched Max gingerly rub his covered erection.

"We've got lots to make up for," Max cooed. His eyes glittered darkly and his lashes lowered with a lusty-lidded look as he climbed up onto the bed in front of her.

"Now it's my turn to take that pretty little mouth of yours, cat." He pressed his thick erection close to her face.

Her mouth instantly watered as she smelled a wonderful scent wafting from the edible thong he wore.

Banana daiquiri. Her absolute favorite drink.

FIVE

*S*HE TOOK A LONG lick and enjoyed the way the material disintegrated. Banana daiquiri flavor exploded against her tongue. Sweet and scrumptious.

She took another swipe. The hole in the fabric got bigger and her tongue found his hot, smooth cock head. A few more wet licks and she had the thong falling off Max.

His erection speared into the air at her. She couldn't help but moan appreciatively at the sight.

His penis appeared even bigger than earlier when they'd been down in Dining Room Seven. The plum-shaped head, swollen and needy. His cock flushed and rigid. She couldn't wait to have him thrusting deep inside of her. She found herself remembering the intense way Max's mouth had suckled earlier on her breasts. Her nipples still ached and she rubbed them back and forth against the edge of the mattress, loving the way every nerve ending sparkled with pleasure.

"You're more than ready, aren't you Allie cat?" Max hissed as he aimed his cock at her mouth.

She nodded numbly and parted her lips. His cock scorched

her like a brand and her jaw ached as she opened wide to accommodate his big size. He tasted of man and lust and she eagerly slurped her tongue along the thick web of veins that ran throughout the length of his stiff shaft.

"Oh yes, that's it, cat. Beautiful. Just fucking beautiful."

His soft guttural compliment made her blood sing. Made her slurp quicker. Made her suck his shaft harder. He groaned his approval and grabbed both sides of her head, trapping her as he took control of her mouth with his cock.

His solid flesh thrust deep and quick.

Silence followed, interrupted by intermittent slaps of flesh against flesh. A moan here, a cry there, as the two men kept a steady erotic rhythm. Her eyelids grew heavy with the haze of arousal from Nick's well-placed tongue strokes to her pussy and Max's plunges into her mouth.

"Sorry, cat, but your teasing licks are just way too much for me," Max growled.

Her fingers gnarled tighter around the sheets as the arousal snowballed. Her thighs tightened. She bucked against Nick and pleasure whipped through her at lightning speed.

She exploded on a scream. The sound a muffled alley-cat screech around Max's thick erection.

"That's it, cat," she heard Max soothe. "Ride the wave."

Violent spasms tore through her, ripping her body apart. Her pussy clenched as Nick removed his tongue and thrust two fingers in and out of her. Tremors gripped her hard and heavy.

All too soon the climax ebbed away. Max pulled out from her mouth and Nick withdrew his fingers.

An aroused after-climax daze drifted over her. She found herself being lifted onto the bed.

"Climb onto me, cat," Max whispered a few seconds later.

She blinked. Hadn't even realized he now lay on the bed beside her. She moaned at the sight of his huge erection. Mewed as she mounted him.

Crouching over his spearing cock, she cried out as she impaled herself on his stiff flesh. Slurping sounds ripped through the air as her vagina greedily clamped around him.

Max groaned hotly. Reaching out, he popped the front clasp, allowing her bra to drop open, then he grabbed her pink nipples. His fingers twisted and pulled until the line of fire screamed into her pussy. She began a mad grind, gyrating her hips, crushing her pussy into his body, then lifting herself and coming down on him, her sheath enveloping his cock again.

In no time flat she had a nice steady rhythm going. Quickly she slipped her finger between her legs and over her swollen clitoris to begin a hard massage.

Ah, this feels wonderful.

She looked down and watched her breasts bounce erotically while Max continued to pull and squeeze her nipples. She saw the perspiration beading Max's forehead. Felt it dot her enflamed body.

Movement to her right made her aware of Nick. He stood beside the bed and through her sexual haze she watched as he greased his turgid penis.

Wow! He looked so huge. It made her remember that she hadn't been anally penetrated for so long. Yet she couldn't wait to feel the pressure of his penis inside her as both men impaled her.

The erotic feeling of having two men double penetrating her. There was nothing else like it on Earth.

Max tugged harder at her nipples and her fingers splayed desperately.

She felt the climax coming and cried out as it rammed into her. She exploded on a scream. Max groaned as her pussy clenched around him. She drew air into her lungs in quick, labored gasps and continued to pump herself over him.

She whimpered as a warm pair of greased hands settled over her shoulders, moving her forward.

"I need to come, kitten. You two look too damned hot."

Nick's lubed finger pressed intimately at her ass. She cried out as the tight ring of sphincter muscles gave way and he slid into her. Pressure bit deep, throwing her off balance.

"So damned tight. Forgot . . . how . . . tight." Nick groaned as he slowed his intrusion. She tried to relax and immediately her anal muscles accepted him. A moment later he slid a second finger inside and began a slow erotic exploration that had her gasping.

"Your ass seems to remember me," he chuckled as a third finger entered. Pleasure-pain burst through her and her muscles eagerly gripped all three digits.

"Very nice," he cooed, and began a thrusting motion that made her squeeze her eyes closed. She panted softly and concentrated on the wonderful buzz starting inside her ass. Before long she was completely relaxed and enjoying the spearing rhythm.

When he withdrew, she opened her eyes and eagerly awaited his next move. A second later his generously lubed cock head slipped into her.

She moaned at the pressure. Fought for breath at the sweet, intense pain.

He bucked his hips and sank deeper. Another thrust had her coming down on Max. Her mouth was inches from his and she suddenly realized they hadn't kissed each other for years. He must have realized the same thing for his eyes grew dark with lust and longing. His mouth parted slightly. She watched him lick his lower lip in a sensual swipe that had her heart skipping a beat.

How in the world could the sight of a man's tongue turn her on so much? But it did. It always did. His hot breath washed against her face breaking her from her fetish.

After years apart, should they not have kissed when they'd first met again? No, her mind reassured her. Kissing came when the time was right.

The time was perfect now.

She caught his mouth and his lips melted against hers. While Max and she explored each other's mouths after such a long absence, Nick began a wonderful thrusting motion. Every plunge forced her clit against Max's hard erection. Another volley of pleasure lanced her.

She shattered and shook as the flames licked her body, screaming into Max's mouth.

Nick plunged deep into her ass. He kept up the demanding thrusts for a delicious eternity. She lay sandwiched between them. Her soaked cunt impaled on Max's cock. Her mouth fused and her ass filled.

The next climax came quickly on the heels of the last. Sweet and oh-so beautifully violent it rushed through her in one hot wave. Within seconds she became lost in yet another brilliant pleasure storm.

MAX HAD NEVER BEEN able to get enough of Allie. Years without her just about made him crazy. Now she was back and the three of them would make up for all the lost time. He was stupid for not going after the woman he loved so badly. When she left, it felt like a knife thrusting deep into his heart.

Pride prevented Max from going after her. Over the years maturity pushed his pride aside and now he felt selfish. The three of them always had great sex and a loving relationship.

This time around he would commit to supporting Allie. Support her as a partner in their personal and professional lives. Why he didn't see it earlier, he had no idea. But now he knew what she needed. It was more than love and sex.

"She's quite a woman, our kitten." Nick grinned from the other side of Allie. Up until now they remained silent as they watched her sleep.

"She taught me a lesson walking away the way she did."

"Knocked sense into you," Nick chuckled.

"I won't be letting her get away again."

"We didn't know what we had until she was gone," Nick echoed his thoughts.

Max read the longing in Nick's eyes when he discovered Allie had walked out on them. He knew Nick loved Allie just as much as he did. Knew he wanted to go after her and bring her home.

But he didn't.

Neither of them did. Deep down they both must have known

she needed space and the two of them needed to realize how much they missed her.

"It was only a matter of time before we hooked up again," Nick stated as he began stroking the length of his quickly hardening shaft. "She needed space to follow her dreams without us hanging all over her. I figured it would only be a matter of time before it sank through your thick skull that she's a jewel, inside and out."

Max nodded in agreement. He was stubborn, he admitted it. Sometimes something drastic had to happen before he came to his senses. And Allie leaving them had been drastic, that's for sure.

He reached down and began toying gently with Allie's exposed nipple. Both men watched as her nipple blushed a deeper shade of pink and hardened into a beautiful rosebud. Nick took her other nipple and pinched it.

She moaned softly and her eyes blinked open. Surprise crossed her face until she realized where she was. Then she smiled. Max could barely breathe at the beautiful sight of their woman looking so happy to see them back in bed with her.

She cocked her head questioningly and watched as they both played with her nipples.

"What are you two guys up to?"

"Ready to purr for us, Allie?" Nick cooed as he brought his mouth over Allie's exposed breast.

Max watched as she hissed and arched her back, making the sheets move lower on her waist until her nude pussy became exposed.

Fuck. She was simply too beautiful to ignore.

"Are you gentlemen ready to roar for me?" she moaned as Max's mouth latched on to her other tight nipple.

Both grinned and nodded in agreement.

Allie made them roar many times that day and for many years after.